CW01514137

Energia's Research Adventures

Perspectives on Renewable Energy and Research Methods

Jacques L. Koko, Ph.D.

BALBOA.PRESS
A DIVISION OF HAY HOUSE

Balboa Press books may be ordered through booksellers or by contacting:

Balboa Press
A Division of Hay House
1663 Liberty Drive
Bloomington, IN 47403
www.balboapress.com
844-682-1282

The views expressed in this work are solely those of the author and do not necessarily reflect the views of the publisher, and the publisher hereby disclaims any responsibility for them.

The author of this book does not dispense medical advice or prescribe the use of any technique as a form of treatment for physical, emotional, or medical problems without the advice of a physician, either directly or indirectly. The intent of the author is only to offer information of a general nature to help you in your quest for emotional and spiritual well-being. In the event you use any of the information in this book for yourself, which is your constitutional right, the author and the publisher assume no responsibility for your actions.

Cover Art by Jacques L. Koko

Print information available on the last page.

ISBN: 979-8-7652-2779-4 (sc)
ISBN: 979-8-7652-2781-7 (hc)
ISBN: 979-8-7652-2780-0 (e)

Library of Congress Control Number: 2022907725

Balboa Press rev. date: 05/30/2022

For Barbara, my loving and lovely wife and friend: our relationship teaches me that getting to know someone or something is a challenging process, it requires renewed efforts day after day and a perpetual recommitment of one's ego (or self) to an alter ego (another self).

To my children Julie, Jacques, and Marie: you remind me that knowledge springs from an active faith in some potential reality, a faith which materializes into a relentless quest or determination to uncover the unknown and bring it into explicit existence.

To all my students, with whom I learn one semester after another that the paths to knowledge are multiple and diverse, and that learning is a daily and lifelong process.

CONTENTS

ACKNOWLEDGMENTS

I thank everyone who participated in the production of this book. Its pages present multiple ways of acquiring knowledge, by casting enlightening perspectives on research methods intertwined with energy sources. By means of storytelling, the book examines non-renewable and renewable energy sources through the lenses of a variety of research methodologies. It sheds light on the meaning of research, portrays different tactics for designing and conducting research in the social sciences, both in quality and quantity, inductively and deductively. It translates the great diversity that research cultures or traditions nestle. It utilizes fiction to discuss a set of qualitative and quantitative research methods for data collection, including the techniques of self-examination, diary or journal keeping, observation, interview, survey, and experiment. It also explains strategies for data analysis that encompass content analysis, narrative analysis, comparative analysis (independent t-test, paired-sample t-test, and one-way analysis of variance), correlation analysis, regression analysis, time-series analysis, and factor analysis.

Energia, the main character of this book, embarks on a comprehensive and substantive research journey to discover and scrutinize the benefits of renewable energies, by using sequences of quantitative and qualitative research methods. Her adventures expose how each research culture hosts a battery of strategies, with strengths and weaknesses or limitations. Her stories illustrate that the qualitative design has a unique ability to be open-ended and to go in depth into revealing the participants' worldviews, experiences, and feelings in the research process and outcome, but this approach often covers a small number of cases, which may not help much policymaking on a macro level or scale. The quantitative procedures are closed-ended, with the potential to cover large scopes in research, which is good news for macro policymaking, but they remain on the surface and fail to account for the participants' deep emotions and other meaningful underlying assumptions. The qualitative methodology explores reality in depth on a narrow scope, but the quantitative method explains reality superficially on a large scope. Both approaches interact fruitfully to exemplify epistemology, with regard to the methods for acquiring knowledge in depth, scope, and validity, through induction and deduction.

In the perspective of this book, no research tradition is better than the other one. Qualitative and quantitative strategies mutually complement and strengthen each other in a dynamic synthesis of mixed methods. Mixed methodology symbiotically builds on the strengths of both qualitative and quantitative research techniques. Scientists humbly acknowledge and resort to the tactical assets of all the research traditions for the success and progress of scientific discoveries, and for reliability and validity in the processes and outcomes of scientific investigations. Chapter by chapter, the stories of the book enhance how the diversity inherent to research methods provides the key for a holistic perspective on scientific knowledge across the human time and space.

Energia's research adventures confirm the significance of diversity and moderation not only in the realm of research methodologies, but also in the human use and history of non-renewable and renewable energies. By means of fiction, the book examines the daunting journey of the humankind through the fossil fuels, solar, wind, and water energy sources in the perspective of yin and yang. The message for the reader is simple. In our quest of answers for the many questions we face daily in existence, we need to balance and embrace diversity and moderation mindfully in the processes and outcomes of our investigations for the sake of a healthy human environment and nature. There may not be any narrow one-size-fits-all solution to the resilient existential issues of energy facing our environment and its species. Existential queries usually imply a broad stream of multiple potential solutions, each of which presents both advantages and disadvantages. Written as a dialogue between a student and a teacher, with the teacher addressing the student's questions and concerns, this book creatively captures and delineates the basics of renewable energies and research methods.

CHAPTER 1

Self-Examination over the Dialectic of Energy Sources

E nergia was born in a very troubled kingdom called Energium. Her father's name was Energon, and Energid was her mother's. The name Energia means energy. Her parents gave her that name symbolically to indicate some unconditional attachment to their cultural origins. Energium was the kingdom of potentials. The kingdom earned its name and fame from its energetic resources, and it took pride in its widespread culture of non-renewable energy sources. In the mainstream life in Energium, the fossil fuels drove the human interactions daily. The coal, petroleum, and natural gas permeated and enabled social activities in that kingdom. Their intensive and extensive use of the fossil fuels had set a tradition addicting most of the citizens of Energium to hydrocarbon fuels.

In a process of self-examination, Energia would become deeply aware of how her existence was molded around and subject to the fossil fuels. As she embarked on the journey of self-evaluation, she reviewed her personal diaries or daily journals for data collection, and her findings about her daily life and existence were telling.

She drove a diesel engine to work every day. On her way to work, she enjoyed listening to YouTube music on her Android phone. As a computer engineer, she spent her workday around and in the cyberspace. She worked in a tremendous data center that ran largely on the fossil fuels. She used plastic bags daily to wrap or pack her lunch for work. At work, she carried around plastic cups for her coffee or beverage. She also relied on the plastic bags for her trash can.

In her workplace and in many organizations across Energium, the lights were on day and night, unnecessarily sometimes, per her own confession. In her neighborhood, Energia could identify public places such as stadiums and concert halls that kept their lights on around-the-clock, needlessly. The lights were on day and night on all the streets and roads of Energium. The kingdom had developed such wasteful habits due to its large power plants, the main emitters of nitrogen dioxide and air pollutants in Energium.

Energia spent her weekends on the phone, texting her friends or calling them on the WhatsApp. She also spent long hours on other social media platforms, including the Facebook, the Instagram, the Twitter, and the YouTube. At times, she spent her weekends helping her mother do the laundry and wash the dishes by relying on their electric dishwasher, laundry machine, and dryer.

Every Christmas, every Easter, and every summer, Energia's family members would get on a plane and head to remote destinations for their vacations.

Every member of her family used an electric toothbrush and operated an electric shaving machine daily. All her relatives relied on electric devices to iron their garments before wearing them.

Her brother Energen was an air traffic controller at the busiest airport in the kingdom; he was fond of cryptocurrency and did most of his transactions digitally in Bitcoin.

Her parents relied on the coal for light in the house and for heating and cooling. They never ran out of hot water because their house had a uniquely enormous water heater. The high capacity of their water heater allowed Energia and everyone in their family to enjoy a long hot shower every morning.

Her mother Energid also relied on gas daily to cook delicious meals for the family. She often resorted to her microwave to warm the leftovers. Energid would carefully store the leftovers in the refrigerator, and freeze whatever required freezing. She spent several hours of her weekend in the kitchen around her stoves and oven for hours of cooking and baking. She cooked while listening to the radio. She also spent hours watching television in the weekend. She worked for a company called Xylion, which ranked first on a global scale in their exploitation of xylene for antiseptics. As a professional accountant, Energid spent the weekdays behind her computer, downloading heavy documents, or creating and storing large files. On her way to work, she enjoyed listening to the radio while driving.

They all relied on petroleum to operate their automobiles. Every member of Energia's family owned a car they drove to work every day. Whenever their cars malfunctioned, they would board the train or the bus to go to work. They thought and behaved as if their workplaces could not function without the coal and petroleum. Most of the organizations in the kingdom of Energium depended on the fossil fuels for power and light. The computer networks or cyber systems of many organizations in the kingdom relied on the fossil fuels for operation.

Energia's father also resorted to the coal or petroleum oil to operate other engines. Every weekend, Energon enjoyed cleaning the carpets in his house with the vacuum cleaner and mowing the yard with his tractor. As a professional developer and builder, he spent his weekdays operating heavy machines to destroy trees and flatten woodlands, wetlands, and farmlands for new constructions.

Energia's self-examination clearly opened her eyes on the benefits of the fossil fuels for herself, her family, her workplace and other organizations, and her country. There was a time she thought they could not live without the fossil fuels.

But she would also become mindful of the disadvantages of the non-renewable sources of energy. She would realize the troubling downsides of the fossil fuels.

In the process of her self-examination, Energia remembered some tragedies in the history book of the kingdom. There were times of major oil spills from ships traveling across Energium. Those oil spills polluted the oceans and beaches of the kingdom, its waters, and its overall environment. They inflicted serious and irreparable damages on the marine ecosystem. They killed many sea creatures, including fish and crabs. Hundreds of birds perished. The spills also contributed to food poisoning; some citizens of Energium died of food poisoning in that period; many others contracted respiratory diseases due to the poor quality of the air they breathed. The air was unbearable for the lungs in some neighborhoods. Those times were disastrous for biodiversity.

There was a time when the long oil pipeline crossing the lands of Energium cracked, and it released oil and lead in the water across the kingdom. Lead poisoning endangered many children's health with autism or attention deficit hyperactivity disorder (ADHD), severely affecting their mental and physical development. The oil leak polluted the drinking water and affected the farming economy of Energium. The disaster impacted the health of many citizens; the most devastating effects manifested in rural communities. It hit the farmers very hard with consecutive years of bad crops and drought in the kingdom.

The correlated issues of water pollution, air pollution, and noise pollution contributed to some harsh crises in the public health, which placed the social life on hold in Energium. They made citizens' lives difficult and put thousands at the edge of the precipice in the kingdom and beyond its borders. Water pollution, air pollution and noise pollution contributed to weakening many citizens' immune systems. Such issues of pollution fostered the emergence and proliferation of new endemics, epidemics, or pandemics such as the Covid-19.

The Covid-19 pandemic was an infectious disease that once halted life and transformed basic social activities and interactions in Energium and beyond. The disease spread fast through a virus called the coronavirus. The speedy and drastic propagation of the coronavirus paralyzed the social interactions to a large extent. The monster of the coronavirus could go from a person to another person through sneezing, coughing, yawning, hugging, kissing, or handshakes. It was mind-boggling to anticipate you could get the coronavirus by shaking people's hands or by giving them a hug. The virus could travel by air on the thin wings of air pollutants. It could also live for days on any surface, including on a paper or plastic.

Apparently, it could infiltrate your mail and you would get it from your mailbox. You could also get it from your grocery, per some speculations.

This public health disaster put an end to the mainstream culture of kisses, hugs, and handshakes; it took away those symbolic gestures of affection and basic physical contacts. It led to the closure of all the schools, workplaces, and places of worship in Energium for months. The hotels, bars, restaurants, and movie theaters also closed for several months. The public transportations also shut down. The airline companies drastically slowed down. The local authorities cancelled or suspended all major sporting events for several months, including the football and basketball games or tournaments. Other specific measures to curb or prevent the spread of the coronavirus called on the citizens to isolate themselves in their homes and to remain distant physically from one another. Renowned hygienists went around the kingdom to remind citizens to wash their hands multiple times a day, to get a minimum of eight hours of sleep at night, and to use the Hindu greeting gesture of "*Namaste*" to greet their neighbors instead of shaking hands.

In that period, long lines of shoppers overcrowded the grocery stores in search of basic food items to survive the long months of a compulsory quarantine. Wearing gloves on their hands, and with their mouths and noses covered with face masks, long chains of citizens invaded retail and wholesale stores of the kingdom. The shoppers emptied the shelves from canned food and fresh food for their subsistence. The high demands from the hungry citizens overwhelmed the food supply chains in Energium, and some items such as beef and milk became rare and expensive in the kingdom. Everybody in the stores wore personal protective equipment (PPE) such as gloves and face masks. Some even wore face shields for protection against the coronavirus. The face masks became an integral part of the dress code. The kingdom made the port of the face masks a requirement for all the citizens. It was a new norm, a new culture for the citizens of Energium.

Across the kingdom, analysts observed a surge in the use of the social media for public or private communication and for group coordination in the same period. The Facebook, Google, Twitter, and YouTube provided citizens with helpful tools to communicate and coordinate social activities in both the public and private sectors. There was a rise in the use of telematics. A large number of organizations would rely on teleconferences so their workers could complete the job from home. Many schools would rely on the Zoom platform, the Remo platform, the Skype, the Microsoft Teams, the Slack, and other similar platforms to teach online. Distant learning got a major boost in that period. Due to overcrowding in the hospitals, there was a surge in the use of telemedicine for patient care.

The coronavirus put the public health system of the kingdom on the verge of collapse. The virus contaminated and killed thousands of citizens. Hundreds of Covid-19 patients overcrowded the hospitals across the lands of Energium. The sweeping virus hit cohorts of health care providers and nurses hard; it decimated many lives in the kingdom. The coronavirus pandemic took away several thousands of lives and millions of jobs. Many citizens lost their neighbors, friends, and relatives. The virus would even not allow those still living to honor their dead with due final respect. At the peak of the crisis, big trucks moved from one street to another to collect dead bodies around-the-clock. One evening, Energia witnessed a truck piled up with dead bodies, moving in her neighborhood, as she traveled to buy some food items from a grocer's store nearby. The horrifying scene traumatized her tremendously.

To avoid the high risks of contagion, and to prevent high rates of contamination, the authorities of Energium put in place strict regulations to rush the bodies to the graves without proper handling, in the absence of big crowds, and without decent burial treatments in some cases. The new policies allowed a strict minimum of people to attend burials. When Energia's coworker Bata lost her father Notu to the coronavirus, the regulations allowed only a total of six people at the burial site, including family members and friends, in addition to the official burial crew.

Many businesses collapsed and filed for bankruptcy, and the economy of the kingdom plummeted and weakened significantly. Many people lost their jobs. The rates of unemployment skyrocketed in every corner of Energium. Citizens became anxious and suspicious. It was a time of great incertitude; you could not plan any social or public event with certitude; the future was very uncertain on all accounts. It was a complete chaos, with the reign of panic and despair all over the kingdom. The crisis culminated in the *Great Resignation*, with massive waves of workers quitting their jobs. The government government of Energium struggled terribly to handle and slow down the coronavirus; it was unchartered territory for all political, medical, and scientific authorities.

Prior to the Covid-19 pandemic, the nationalist king of Energium had allocated billions in funding (including the money initially dedicated to the management of disasters such as pandemics) to build a wall to protect the borders of his kingdom against the immigrations from neighboring countries. However, in the wake of the magnitude and severity of the coronavirus, the king would realize his mistake. He understood his kingdom needed not to build walls. Instead, they needed money to support or revitalize existing hospitals, to build new ones, and to buy critical medical equipment such as protective masks, gloves, and ventilators to save citizens' lives in the midst of a dire crisis of public health.

Eventually, assiduous scientists would discover a set of vaccines against the coronavirus, to prevent and slow down the spread of the monstrous disease. The discovery would save millions of lives in the kingdom and beyond its borders.

As she continued her self-examination, Energia seemed to understand that water pollution, air pollution, and noise pollution also had some impacts on global warming and climate change. During the Covid-19 pandemic, the metropolises or megalopolises of the kingdom, with the highest rates of air pollution and noise pollution, had the highest rates of coronavirus infections. The high rates of nitrogen dioxide in the air were unhealthy for the lungs; they could not help the lungs resist the coronavirus. The noise from the ambulances and other heavy engines did not foster restful nights and mental health relief for the residents. The rural areas of Energium, with the lowest rates of air pollution and noise pollution, had the lowest Covid-19 rates or barely recorded any case of coronavirus infection. The air quality was cleaner in the countryside in Energium, and the residents could breathe better; the lack of noise was conducive to a better quality of sleep and restful nights.

As the coronavirus waged a disastrous war on Energium, the government ordered all the citizens to stay at home to observe a general lockdown or quarantine to curb the spread of the virus. During that mandatory lockdown the kingdom observed a drastic drop in air pollution. There was no smog in the sky of Energium, and for the first time, some citizens were able to see the horizon clearly in their neighborhoods, because there were less cars on the roads and many factories were closed. This was a great opportunity for some residents to get their best air quality in decades in many regions of the kingdom. This brought good news for healthy lungs, amid the coronavirus pandemic.

Energia recalled some dramatic severe weathers in the kingdom. Dozens of harsh hurricanes or cyclones had hit Energium in recent years, and they had caused the losses of thousands of human lives. The kingdom had also recorded a large number of devastating earthquakes and tsunamis that took the lives of many citizens.

She also remembered some years of frequent and fierce explosions of oil tankers traveling throughout Energium. Those explosions had triggered ferocious wildfires that ravaged villages and killed records of citizens, including her friends and relatives. The ecosystem took the biggest hit. The fires destroyed the wildlife, killing thousands of animals and destroying beautiful forests and other natural sites. The country recorded some massive destructions of its botanical and zoological gardens in that period. The citizens of Energium felt the negative impacts of the fires on tourism; the sequels were very noticeable across the kingdom.

Energia's self-reflection would move on to contemplate how the fossil fuels had fostered some destructive dynamics of greed and conflicts in many places in Energium and beyond its borders, across the time and space. The historical records of the kingdom showed how it had often engaged in violent conflicts with its rivals over petroleum oil. One of the cruelest wars between the kingdom of Energium and the kingdom of Energol was over who should control the oil wells in the small kingdom of Energan. The two big kingdoms coveted the oil wells of Energan, and they wanted to exercise a mutually exclusive control over the small kingdom. The king of Energan faced a difficult dilemma in deciding on a side. If he were to side with Energium, he would lose the friendship of the kingdom of Energol. If he were to side with Energol, this would affect his people's relationship with the kingdom of Energium. Regardless of his decision, it would affect the interests of his kingdom. He did not want to disappoint either party. Therefore, he called on all the stakeholders to negotiate for win-win outcomes for all three kingdoms. Trapped by greedy ambitions to control the oil wells fully and selfishly, the two major parties were unable to negotiate over their mutual interest. They waged a harsh war that killed thousands of citizens in Energium, Energol, and Energan. At the end of the war, many citizens in Energium, including Energia, put the blame on petroleum oil. Petroleum oil had fueled a large number of cruel wars around the globe.

Energia's method of self-examination raised her awareness about the perilous impacts of the human beings' immoderate usages of the fossil fuels. She thought, "Despite the advantages they offer, the fossils fuels also jeopardize the human existence; they present several disadvantages and threats to the humankind. They contaminate our water, pollute the air, and damage our environment; they contribute to global warming and climate change."

She would ask herself, "What are some alternatives to the coal and fossil fuels?"

In an attempt to find answers to that pertinent question, she decided to expand her self-examination to encompass a historical review of energy sources in the olden days. She chose to examine her ancestors' culture of energy use, the culture that was before the culture of the coal and fossil fuels.

Energia's expansive self-examination led her to contemplate and compare her era to her ancestors' epoch. She engaged in an extensive historical review of her ancestor Energius' journals over the sources of energy in the time and space. She would carefully spend several days in that endeavor. In the night that followed the first day of her intensive review of Energius' journals, Energia had an interesting dream while sleeping. The dream took her to the olden days of her ancestors. In her dream, she engaged in a very productive conversation with Energius over how his generation had used energy. Energius had lived as a farmer in a very rural Energium five hundred years ago.

Without any preparation or notes, Energia initiated a typical unstructured interview with Energius. With no written questions beforehand, she informally and spontaneously inundated her interviewee with a series of questions on her mind about energy sources in the olden days.

"What were the main sources or forms of energy in your epoch?" she asked Energius excitedly.

"In those days," he replied elatedly, "we relied on the sun, the wind, water, and the wood as the main sources for our moderate use and need of energy. Most of the citizens of Energium would count on the sun for light and heat. The sunlight rhythmed our schedules and activities; we woke up with the sunrise and went to bed with the sunset. We would start our daily activities at dawn, and we stopped working at dusk; we would not work at night."

"On sunny days," he continued mindfully, "my family would open our windows to allow enough sunshine inside to keep the house warm. After washing our clothes with her hands, my lovely wife Energes would spread them on the grass outside in the open air, counting on the sunlight to dry them thoroughly. There was no electric washer or dryer."

"In the absence of the sunlight," he went on fervently, "we would burn the firewood for heat and light. We used the wood to cook our food, to heat our houses, and to make fire for visibility at night. At times, my Energes would also burn the dried dung from our cows. Additionally, a huge peat on the farmstead often supplied us with fuel for basic needs."

Energia was all ears, but she thought his ancestor's perspectives were mind-bending.

"How did you use energy in your activities?" she interrupted Energius impatiently.

"As a farmer," he explained patiently, "I first relied on the human labor, my muscles and the assistance I got from other human beings, including my family and relatives, my neighbors, and my friends. I also resorted to the help of my cows, donkeys, and horses for heavier or harder farming activities and for the transportation of my people and goods."

"My generation," he continued passionately, "depended on the wind for navigating across the rivers and oceans, and for fishing. I relied on the power of the wind to operate my windmill to grind corn and millet, to pump water for the farm, and to generate electricity. At times, I would also count on water and the power of the steam to operate my machine for grinding grain into flour for my family's subsistence. Whenever my windmill failed, I resorted to the waterwheel on the river running past the farmstead to generate power for the farm. In the winter, we would harvest ice from the millpond and store it in the icehouse to preserve perishable food. There was no electric refrigerator. Ice cutting was a traditional activity in our family. It was very fun."

"Were you aware of what the levels of carbon emissions were in those olden days?" Energia interjected again sharply.

"Ours was an age of a lower carbon economy or market," he replied proudly, "the levels of carbon emissions in Energium were significantly low; we were mindful of the environment."

In the dream and interview process, Energia became aware that the people from her ancestors' era had lived happier; their stress levels were extremely low. They had rarely experienced anxiety or depression; they did not record high rates of illnesses such as cancer and pulmonary or cardiovascular diseases. In those years, the citizens of Energium lived in a virgin and naturally sane environment despite the lack of scientific advancements in that period. Their lifestyle in terms of energy use was sober or modest. Many of them enjoyed a long life, including Energius.

She kept listening to Energius with admiration as he said, "Based upon my life experience and after navigating different cultures, I see everything through cultural lenses, including the current debate the young generations have over climate change and renewable energy."

"Can you clarify what you mean?" she asked him insistently.

Energius took a deep breath and explained, "Per my observations and experiences," he said persuasively, "every transition in energy type has correlated with a social revolution. Historically, the sunlight, the firewood, the wind and water were the first sources of energy for the human beings. The transition to coal triggered the industrial revolution with resounding social, structural, and systemic changes and adjustments. The shift to oil and natural gas has contributed to geo-political changes and global conflicts. The transition to nuclear energy has been harmful to the public health and threatened the survival of the humankind in my opinion."

"The switch from the fossil fuels back to renewable energies such as solar energy, wind energy, moving water energy, and geothermal energy," he continued cogently, "will transform social relations tremendously. But that change might not imply a complete turnabout for the human use of the fossil fuels. To some extent, your generation might still need to rely on some fossil fuels to make the equipment for wind energy or the devices for the solar panels, and in other human activities. You might still need to count on the fossil fuels, due to your addiction to a digital economy that implies high volumes of downloading and streaming. The digital economy certainly requires some excessive usages of energy."

Energia listened with interest, and she begged her ancestor to say more.

"I am aware of a fact," he went on majestically, "there are ferocious debates over the right course of action for addressing the global warming and climate change. I know the tensions are high between the proponents of renewable energies and their opponents. Each camp claims to have the right solution, and both camps lock themselves in a game of scapegoating, instead of engaging in a constructive dialogue for a shared accountability over the pressing issues, to agree on mutually acceptable solutions."

"As I contemplate the human history across the time and space," he continued diligently, "I approach the debate on the global warming, climate change and renewable energy in light of multiculturalism. Energy is multicultural; it radiates a multicultural connotation and adjusts to a battery of cultural or social decorum. Each culture, generation, or type of energy has its strengths and limitations; we should not overuse the non-renewable energies, because they could run out, and overusing them contributes to global warming and climate change. However, we need to be realistic in the transition from non-renewable energies to renewable energies."

"Per my observation," he persisted meticulously, "it is not your intake of a prescribed medication that is a problem, the right dose of the medication will not kill you; the problem comes from the amount of that medication you take. If you take more than your body can handle, you might hurt your body and jeopardize your life. By analogy, the main source of the climate problem comes from the exclusively large amounts of fossil fuels the human beings currently consume with the correlating high emissions of carbon. Your generation consumes too much fossil fuels, you consume far more than your natural environment can handle. The people of this age need to manage their addiction to hydrocarbon fuels and cut down their consumption of the fossil fuels drastically; they largely need to integrate alternative options from renewable energies."

"I encourage you," he exhorted Energia soundly, "to conduct some research on renewable, clean, or green energy. Participant observations, interviews, surveys, and experiments will allow you to collect primary data to assess the benefits of renewable energy for the human health and the natural environment. If non-renewable energies seem to provide a thesis for the human energy use for the people of your generation, be mindful that renewable energies can represent a safe and healthy antithesis in terms of energy sources for your age. Neither source of energy (non-renewable or renewable) could pretend to represent exclusively a fully satisfactory option for the human needs in energy. With all their advantages, non-renewable energies pollute the environment and contribute to global warming and climate change. Despite a large number of undeniable benefits, renewable energies alone might not be able to meet sufficiently the insatiable demands and hunger for energy in your epoch; renewable energies certainly have their shortcomings. The dialectic of the human historical records suggests that the reasonable solution might not be exclusively in the thesis or the antithesis. The judicious solution might reside in the synthesis, a moderate and reasonably balanced combination of non-renewable and renewable energies. The tensions between the thesis in non-renewable energies and their antithesis in renewable energies resolve in the synthesis of a moderate mixture."

Following the self-examination and the conversation with her ancestor, Energia experienced deep feelings of guilt, after she had woken up from her dream. She felt guilty of contributing to harming her natural environment with some of her actions or choices. She felt her extreme and constant reliance on the fossil fuels would contribute to the progressive destruction of the planet. She instantaneously made the decision no longer to board a plane; she immediately thought of giving up her car. She also thought of stopping using plastic and downloading documents or streaming videos.

But she would quickly realize that none of those short-term emotional resolutions could grant her sustainable peace of mind and heart. She found it hard to give up driving a car. She was able to reduce and regulate her use of plastic, yet she was not successful in repressing completely her needs in plastic. She resolved to think strategically for effectiveness and sustainability, mindful of Energius' invitation to collect and analyze qualitative and quantitative data on renewable energy. She made up her mind to explore, examine, and discover a reality she did not know much about, the matter of renewable energies.

After she had made the decision to study the topic of renewable energies, Energia took some time to consult with her research advisor. His name was Chercheur. He was a distinguished research consultant in the kingdom of Energium.

Energia updated him on the findings of her self-examination, and she unveiled her intention to carry on further research on renewable energies. Chercheur listened to her deeply, and he understood and appreciated her initiative.

"What a great initiative!" he exclaimed. "Our world needs that type of research so much for relevant knowledge on that topic."

"Knowledge," he pursued eloquently on a philosophical route, "hosts aspects of reality and grants you some access to them. Research operationalizes an inexhaustible thirst and quest for knowledge. The research process begins from the moment you identify or select a topic or issue for investigation. Once you choose a topic, you need to define clearly the keywords, formulate a transparent research question, and come up with a hypothesis (if necessary).

"It is helpful how you have started your data collection both preemptively and proactively, with the resourceful technique of self-examination as a groundbreaking research method. Self-examination makes you open the book of your existence to read the pages of your daily activities or interactions with yourself and with other selves. In the process, it makes you listen to yourself profoundly; and as you listen to yourself, you also listen to others around you deeply, because you are situated in relation to others. It is a reliable technique for collecting qualitative and quantitative data, because it allows you to observe, interview, and survey yourself as a human being in relation to you and your social environment."

Chercheur would advise Energia methodically to take the time to conduct a literature review on the benefits of renewable energies. Patiently, he took her on as an apprentice to inspire, guide, and enlighten her steps in the complex process of conducting research.

"What is a literature review?" she asked him, with an excitement that intermingled with curiosity.

"A literature review," he said feverishly, "is an evaluative report you write on a series of studies previously published on your topic. It is a process of examining or scrutinizing what different scholars have written on your topic, an attempt to check their perspectives and listen to their voices over how they conducted their research, what they found, and to hear their implicit or explicit calls for more research on the topic."

"What do you mean by an evaluative report in this context?" she interpolated swiftly.

"An evaluate report is," he answered forcefully, "a written account that displays the strengths and limitations of the research others scholars have conducted and published on your topic."

"How or where do I identify the strengths of what they have written?" asked Energia desperately.

"You identify the strengths," he said convincingly, "in the methods they used for data collection and analysis, and in the results or findings of their studies."

"Could you be more specific about what I should highlight as the strengths of their methods?" she persisted passionately.

Chercheur took a deep breath, looked at Energia, and said in a gentle tone, "Carefully highlight the design of the study, whether it is qualitative, quantitative, or mixed methods, the procedures or techniques the study utilized (observation, interview, survey, experiment, narrative study, content analysis, historical review, review of documents, or archives), the sample size (the specific number of participants in the study), the sampling technique (whether the study selected the participants randomly or not)."

"What about the limitations?" she interposed rapidly.

"The limitations," he replied ardently, "are in the lacks you identify in the methods of previous studies on the topic, or what is shaky in their findings. The limitations reflect the gap in the research, which triggers, announces, or traces new research avenues or paths, and requires new investigations. That gap justifies your research to some extent; it frames the originality of your contribution to the debate on the topic."

"How do I go about doing the literature review in practice? What is the process like, step by step?" she asked eagerly.

"You first need to identify the keywords from your topic and research question, and conduct a library search!" exclaimed Chercheur.

"Would you please explain what you mean?" she went on, unsatisfied.

"Once you are on the website of a library," he said reassuringly, "identify the databases, and open any database of your choice, for instance the *Academic Search Ultimate* or the *JSTOR*. Type your keywords in the respective windows and use the Boolean operators to connect the keywords for your search. The AND operator is to narrow your search, the OR operator is to broaden your search. The NOT operator is to exclude."

"What happens next?" she interrupted impatiently.

"Depending on your topic and the databases," he explained patiently, "your search would generate dozens, hundreds, or thousands of results, including scholarly articles, books, and other documents."

"That is a large number of documents," said Energia anxiously. "What specific types of articles do I or could I retain for my literature review?"

"Do not worry," reassured Chercheur, with a smile. "Ideally," he explained, "you need to focus on peer-reviewed journal articles (also called refereed journal articles); per my experience peer-reviewed articles often present their methods more clearly and more rigorously than books or other documents, and research experts review thoroughly and censor them prior to publication. In many cases, books tend to be less rigorous scientifically or methodologically. They often cast subjective narratives or random essays lacking clear and rigorous scientific methods. Pursuant to your topic and interests, you may add a few books and other documents, if they are transparent in presenting their methods, but I would highly recommend that you primarily opt for scholarly articles from peer-reviewed or refereed journals. Scholarly articles would help you more in identifying the methods for data collection and analysis."

"How many peer-reviewed journal articles should I assess for my literature review in this case?" she asked him enthusiastically.

He observed a moment of silence and explained. "Listen," he said cautiously, "depending on your topic, how much time you have for your research, and other contextual, operational, or structural factors, you could review more or less than fifty peer-reviewed articles, by examining the strengths in the methods they utilized and their results, and the limitations in terms of the gaps.

"Notice," he went on majestically, "I tend to shy away (as much as I can) from advising what you should do; instead, I advise what you could do, because nothing is perfect in science; there are no perfect ways of carrying a scientific investigation; there is always some room for flexibility and improvement in the social sciences. In scientific research, the levels of confidence often rotate around ninety-five percent, leaving about a five percent margin for error. That is why the vaccines scientists discovered against Covid-19 would prevent many recipients from getting sick with Covid-19, while a few others may still get sick after receiving the vaccines. The vaccines are not one hundred percent effective; they cannot be perfect, that is science. Science requires humility.

"Advising in the matter of *what you should do*," he persisted magnificently, "would challenge the notions of imperfection and humility inherent to scientific research. *What you should do* often narrows down, reduces, or limits your options, whereas *what you could do* usually broadens or multiplies your options. Be mindful that *what you could do* is empowering, as it presents you with many possibilities and expands your horizon, while *what you should do* can be disempowering for the self, as it limits your choices by dictating only a few or one. The perspective of *what you could do* inspires the researcher with multiple avenues for learning outcomes; it enables and empowers cultural diversity in the research process and outcome."

While Chercheur kept on explaining, Energia listened carefully, and she took detailed notes. In the end, she said with satisfaction, "I greatly appreciate how you explain the distinction between what I should do and what I could do; your explanation is an eye-opener, it is very helpful."

She would move on quickly, with a follow-up question.

"What would the writing techniques look like in practice as I write the literature review?" she asked keenly.

"Look," he said warmly, "you would summarize and synthesize the articles, by using the past tense."

Energia looked straight at him and asked politely, "Could you provide some specific guidelines on how to write the summary of an article?"

"As I have implied previously," answered Chercheur assertively, "the summary shows the strengths and limitations of the article in terms of its methods for data collection and analysis and the findings. Specifically, it presents the location of the study, its participants, its sample size, its sampling techniques, its results, and its shaky aspects or the gap that new research would fill. Just like a reporter presenting the news, you report what those studies achieved, how they achieved it, and the areas of improvement calling for more research. Using the past tense and the active voice, you recount, narrate, or describe how the article did what it did, its results or what it found, and what needs further research. In the process, you give credit to the authors by mentioning their last names and the year of publication of the article, following consistently the *American Psychological Association* (APA) style, the *Chicago Manual of Style*, the Harvard referencing style, or any other relevant style for proper credits."

"What about the synthesis? How do I write it?" she asked relentlessly.

"The synthesis," he said, "would identify common themes, denominators, or rubrics to regroup or organize the summaries of articles. For instance, you could organize the summaries of the articles you review by looking at the precedents of renewable energies, the manifestations of renewable energies, and the outcomes of renewable energies. You could also choose to synthesize the summaries chronologically; it means you would organize your literature review by regrouping the articles per year or decade of publication. You could start, for example, with the articles written in the 1980s on the topic, and the articles written in the 1990s, followed by those written in the 2000s, and the articles written in the 2010s, and ending with the articles written in the 2020s."

"You would use the last paragraph of the review," he added brilliantly, "to expose briefly the gap in the existing literature and describe how your study intends to fill that gap, by specifying the methods you plan to utilize in terms of the sample size, the sampling technique, the location of your study for primary data collection, and your tools for data analysis. You need to ensure this paragraph is brief; it serves as a transition to announce the method section of your research."

"Could you provide any additional tips to make the writing of the literature review easy?" she asked, bursting out of laughing.

"Certainly!" exclaimed Chercheur, with a smile that seemed to reflect his satisfaction with Energia's progress.

"Per my experience," he said happily, "a well written peer-reviewed article would usually present an abstract at the beginning of the article. A well written abstract reflects most of the components of a good summary of the article. Take your time to read the abstract carefully."

In addition to the supervision she got from Chercheur, Energia would consult a couple of librarians for more technical assistance to hone her writing skills. She would also seek guidance from a number of textbooks on how to write a literature review. She watched a series of relevant Youtube videos on the tips for writing a good literature review. She also would learn from how the authors had organized the literature reviews in the articles she read for writing her own literature review.

Following Chercheur's advice and other related guidelines, she would go ahead and write a comprehensive and pertinent literature review on renewable energies. In the process of the review, her library search resulted in a very large number of peer-reviewed articles and books on the topic. The existing literature on renewable energies was prolific and manifold. Mindful of her research advisor's guidelines, she selected fifty relevant scholarly articles from refereed journals. She would read some articles entirely and skim others. In the reading process, she developed a chronological framework by regrouping the articles written in the 1990s, the ones written in the 2000s, those written in the 2010s, and the ones written in the 2020s. She would use that framework to synthesize her summaries by showing the strengths, the limitations, and the gaps in the articles. She used the last paragraph of the review to explain clearly the hole in the literature, which her research would fill, and how she would close that gap by collecting and analyzing primary data in specific locations and using specific random samples.

She found the process of writing the literature review both challenging and rewarding. It was draining and time-consuming. After completing her literature review, she felt exhausted by the task load involved in searching and reading scholarly articles for summarizing and synthesizing. But she also felt happy about what she had learned. As she read, summarized, and synthesized the articles, she got useful scientific lessons on the natures and benefits of renewable energies. She would confide to Chercheur gratefully, "It was a helpful and worthwhile learning process."

Her conversations with Energius and Chercheur respectively, and the literature review she had written on the topic would reassure her that renewable energies could represent good alternatives to non-renewable energies. Her goal was to investigate what could be their benefits for the humankind.

Her research question was clear and appropriate as she framed it:

"What are some benefits of renewable energies for the humans and their natural environment?"

Her hypothesis was straightforward:

"Renewable energies offer a number of benefits for the humans and their natural environment."

In her strategic planning, she decided to cooperate fully with environmental forces, with the intention of advocating for solar energy, wind energy, and water energy to salvage the environment from degradation and counter global warming or climate change, for the sake of the humankind. She designed an impressive research proposal to uncover the benefits of renewable energies for the human nature and our environment through a series of research strategies, including participant observations, structured and semi-structured interviews, surveys, experiments, and other suitable research methods.

In order to achieve the ambitious goals of her research project, Energia would take a number of judicious measures. She would take a long leave of absence from her workplace for four months. The research project was so dear to her heart; she was aflame with curiosity. Mindful of her project, she had saved enough money to spend six months without pay. She would also apply for a research grant to cover all expenses relating to her research project.

She targeted a series of sites for data collection. The first major stop in her vast operation of data collection would be in a bright or sunny place called Sun City. Her research design would take her to that wonderful city of the solar panels for qualitative observations, in an attempt to learn about the benefits of the solar panels for the human life and environment. Her ultimate goal was to contribute to a lower carbon economy for justice to the universe, in the interest of the humankind.

CHAPTER 2

Energia's Ethnographic Observations

While planning her trip to Sun City, Energia spent some time revisiting and reorganizing some sections of her research proposal. Notably, she would dedicate a large number of hours to polishing the introduction to make a good impression on the readers, for she thought to herself:

"The introduction is like a photo identification of the whole research proposal, the part that announces or reflects the entire body of the research proposal. It deserves to be clean and clear."

In the introduction of her research proposal, she clearly stated the issues involving non-renewable and renewable energies, and she explained their significance by supporting her statements with statistical and scholarly evidence in an attempt to make a strong case. She also stated the purpose and delimitations of her study by specifying the locations of her study, the populations she would target, her sample sizes, and her random sampling techniques; she also described the participants in terms of their age, gender, profession, and other relevant characteristics.

Her introduction also announced her literature review briefly (like in a snapshot), by presenting a small number of existing theories on her topic, anent their methods and findings or conclusions, and the originality her study would add to the existing literature. At the end of the introduction, she framed her research questions as open-ended and closed-ended. She would supply her closed-ended questions with related hypotheses (showing clear independent and dependent variables.) She would define her variables by explaining how she would measure them (as nominal, ordinal, or interval-ratio) to meet the requirements of quantitative research. Her open-ended questions would fulfill the needs of qualitative research.

Energia took some time to consult with her mentor for more advice over the structure of her research questions, and for guidance about how to behave in the entire process of her research.

Mr. Chercheur would help her understand more clearly the difference between closed-ended questions and open-ended ones.

"Closed-ended questions," he said, "present a specific and rigid range of concise answers or options a respondent must select from (for instance, the options of *yes*, *no*, or *maybe*). Meanwhile, open-ended questions allow the respondents to provide flexible, original, and detailed answers reflecting their experiences and feelings."

He would also raise her awareness about potential ethical issues in the research process and outcome, and he would coach her diligently and accordingly.

"The research process and outcome," he warned her patiently and firmly, "will empower you with knowledge as you get helpful information on your topic. It may also empower you with money, if you get a grant for your investigations, or when the outcome of the research results in lucrative or financial gains. Be mindful not to use the power or the privilege of your knowledge or the power of money against the participants in your research. Do not manipulate the people involved in the process."

"What do you mean?" she asked warily. "Please clarify your point."

"Use the power or privilege of knowledge and money to serve the people who participate in your research," he replied punctually.

Energia tilted her head towards Chercheur to show she was much interested in the conversation.

"How do I serve those who take part in my research?" she asked him in a sober tone.

"By respecting them, by keeping their identities confidential if they request confidentiality, by showing integrity and reciprocity, and by being trustworthy and credible," he answered promptly.

"Can you, please, explain further those concepts?" she asked pleadingly.

Chercheur paused for a few seconds before he said, "You respect the participants by framing your research questions politely, and by interacting with the human targets humbly, without being manipulative, judgmental, or arrogant in the processes of observations, interviews, or surveys. For confidentiality, you could use pseudonyms, if the respondents do not want the research to feature their names. Be transparent by making them aware of the purpose of your study and its potential risks for participants."

He would continue by saying, "At every step of the research process, be mindful to ask yourself the following question: do I exercise my power in the perspective of a power for people, or as a power against people? For a power for people is a power with people, it empowers you and others. A power against people is a power over people, it tends to dominate, subjugate or alienate others."

"How about the notion of reciprocity?" she interrupted. "Can you explain what that is all about?"

Chercheur smiled, nodded, and replied, "In the process of data collection, participants give you information relevant to your research. You need to give them something in return. What you give them in return could be money if you get a grant for rewarding them financially; but it does not have to be money. Some participants might ask you to reward them by publishing their names or pictures in the published outcome of the research. That is reciprocity."

"How do I develop credibility and build trust in the process of my research?" she asked insistently.

Apparently thirsty, Chercheur stretched his right hand, reached out to the cup of beverage nearby and took a sip of water before saying, "When the participants trust you, they want to participate in the research and give you pertinent data. If they do not trust you, they do not want to take part in it, or they do not share accurate or relevant information. Disclosing your identity and that of the organization sponsoring or mentoring your research would boost your credibility and help build trust to some degree. In addition, you need to be approachable and show compassion."

"Would you advise any tangible way the research process could reflect all those ethical issues to give the participants some guarantee it will address them ethically?" she asked unrelentingly.

"Certainly!" he exclaimed, "I would advise the researcher to develop an informed consent form, and to hand a copy of it to each participant for reviewing and signing prior to collecting data. That form would explain clearly the purpose of the research, and how the study would handle all such ethical issues relating to respect, confidentiality, reciprocity, benefits for the participants, and potential known risks. Each participant and the researcher would sign the informed consent form prior to data collection to reflect their mutual agreement to participate in the research process. This form protects the participant and the researcher."

"What if a participant changes their mind and decide not to participate in the process after signing the consent form?" she persisted with another follow-up question.

"Ideally, the informed consent will reassure the participants that they can withdraw anytime they decide to withdraw from the study," He explained softly.

Apparently happy with her advisor's explanations, Energia smiled and said, "Your advice is enlightening, but how do we enforce all those ethical rules in research?"

"That is a great question!" he replied excitedly. "There is an independent ethics committee called institutional review board (IRB). The IRB acts like a police station that enforces the ethical rules in research. The IRB reviews and checks research proposals to ensure they do not harm human subjects. The IRB would approve research proposals that are ethically sound or not harmful, and it would disapprove those with the potential to hurt human subjects. Most organizations would have in place an institutional review board. Prior to collecting data, researchers would submit their proposals to the IRB for review and approval."

Energia would go further, by making her advisor clarify his stance on the levels of measurement of variables.

"I struggle with the levels of measurement of my variables," she confessed, "any explanation would be helpful."

"From my perspective, a variable could be measured as nominal, ordinal, or interval-ratio."

"What are some criteria for each level?" she asked.

"The nominal level," he answered, "fits any variable you can break into groups or categories with labels or name tags on. You could also call it a categorical variable, a discontinuous variable, or a grouping variable. Religion would be a nominal variable, because you could classify it as Hinduism, Buddhism, Daoism, Indigenous Beliefs, Voodoo, Judaism, Christianity, Islam, and more. Color is a nominal variable, because it could be black, blue, green, orange, purple, red, yellow, white, and more. Political party is also a nominal variable, because it could be democratic, republican, independent, and more. All such groups call for some random numerical coding; order does not matter on this level."

"What about the ordinal level?" she asked.

"The ordinal level," he replied, "encompasses any variable that you can arrange into ranks, in a specific and rigid order. You could also call it a ranking variable. The size of T-shirt would be an ordinal variable, because it could be small, medium, large, extra-large, and more. Social class is an ordinal variable, because it could be lower, middle, and upper. All such ranks require some rigid and logic numerical coding. You also could consider this level categorical, but a logic order matters here."

"How about the interval-ratio level?" she persisted.

"The interval-ratio level," he said, "includes any variable that comes in numerical values (with no requirement for coded values). You could also call it a numerical variable or a continuous variable. Examples on this level includes age, income, height, length, weight, temperature, miles per hour, and more."

Following their expansive conversation, Energia spent a few days refining her research proposal with Chercheur's assistance. Mindful of her advisor's guidelines, she would develop a robust informed consent form to explain the purpose of her research and how she would address potential ethical issues with deontology. She would refine her research proposal to make it rigorous ethically, to Chercheur's satisfaction. She would get a timely approval from the IRB of Chercheur's academic institution.

Eventually, she also got the good news of the approval of the grant she had applied for to cover the expenses relating to the research project, which was a cause for celebration. She recorded an increase in her eagerness to embark on the journey of her research project. The news of the grant was uplifting, it boosted her motivation, and she was overjoyed.

Three weeks later, Mr. Chercheur moved on to introduce Energia to a friend, the gatekeeper of Sun City. His name was Ethnography.

As she approached the gatekeeper, Energia greeted him politely and introduced herself with the purpose of her visit.

"Welcome to Sun City!" he replied to her. "My name is Ethnography. I study the cultures of peoples, nations, groups, associations, or organizations, and I coach visitors and researchers on how to observe and manage cultural assets and differences. Mr. Chercheur, your mentor, often relies on my services."

Mr. Ethnography spent some time coaching Energia on core cultural requirements of Sun City apropos of good manners and social decorum.

In the coaching process, Energia clarified her intention to collect data on the usage and benefits of solar panels in Sun City. She asked Ethnography, "What technique would best fit or serve my data collection process? Which method would you advise me to use to collect some helpful information?"

After praising Energia for her relevant question, he said, "I am afraid we may not be able to speak in terms of the technique that best fits; it is difficult to measure or quantify what is best. We may speak in terms of what technique is the most appropriate for your research. In this case, one procedure comes to mind, participant observation would be the most appropriate method for your data collection here."

"I do not understand what you mean," she said immediately.

She asked him, "What do you mean by participant observation? How does it work?"

Mr. Ethnography would answer her twofold question by pondering his words. He said gently, "In my worldview, participant observation would make you spend a good amount of time collecting data on solar panels, while staying and mingling with the citizens of Sun City. As a participant observer, you will be working with the people of the city, you will be eating with them, and you will be dancing and playing with them. You will be collecting data as you observe citizens in their day-to-day life; this requires your complete immersion in their daily activities."

"You may reframe participant observation merely," he went on, "as a qualitative method for getting to know social reality, by actively watching and partaking in the observees' activities and lifestyle."

"How do I record the data in those conditions?" she spoke up.

"You can select to take formative notes if the citizens you observe consent," he answered. "Formative notes are the ones you take during the process of your field observations, as they unfold. This implies that you have the targeted participants sign a consent form prior to your observations."

"This could be a challenge," replied Energia anxiously, "it could be difficult to focus on observing people and taking notes at the same time."

Ethnography said, "It could be difficult, but not impossible. Research does not accept anything is impossible to find out. What you cannot figure out today, you will discover it tomorrow, or someone else will help discover it. Research unlocks doors that may look impossible to open, and it uncovers the world of possibilities hiding behind them, for the sake of scientific progress. You may transcend the challenge, if you select to make summative notes. Summative notes are the notes you make after your observations, at the end of the day, before bedtime."

"There could be a challenge as well!" exclaimed Energia impetuously. "If I have to wait till the evening, I may forget some details of my observations by the end of the day."

"You make a good point," he said to her instinctively, "we may forget. The research process cannot be perfect; there is no perfect research. Every research has its limitations. I am afraid no researcher is able to anticipate, prevent, and solve the puzzle of all limitations in their research. As a researcher, you need to be mindful of the limitations of your research and do what you can to alert your readers on them. The mindfulness of the limitations of their research would make the researchers humble. As for you, try as hard as you can to remember the basics of your notes in this situation."

"What alternatives do we have to taking notes?" she asked impulsively.

"You could select to tape-record or videotape your observations, if the people you observe consent to it," he replied. "Every option requires the participants' formal consent."

"What option would you recommend?" she persisted.

"Every option has its advantages and disadvantages," he answered ponderingly. "The decision to select an option depends on series of factors, including issues of the researcher's personality, the informants' preferential option, and the needs of the research. I must confess I have a bias here; I am more inclined to taking notes; it is cheap and handy to make notes. I think the notes would serve the goals of your research conveniently, in spite of the real challenges they could present at times."

Following the coaching session, Mr. Ethnography walked with Energia to the City Hall where he introduced her to the Chief Executive Officer of Sun City, Mr. Sun, another gatekeeper and key informant.

Mr. Sun welcomed Energia warmly in his spacious office. They spent some time chatting on the goal of her visit in Sun City. He lauded her interest in Sun City. "We appreciate your interest in Sun City," he said, "your visit honors our city greatly."

As a telling symbol, he handed a key of the city to Energia to allow her to unlock every door and to have access to every household and office in Sun City for data collection.

He would entertain her on how he supplied his city with the sunlight throughout the year to meet the citizens' needs in renewable energy. He would boast about the large solar power plants his city had put in place for electricity.

"Here, our energy source never dries up," he said proudly, "we never run out of it, it is inexhaustible; it is also cheap."

He went on happily to unveil to his guest the annual budget of Sun City on solar panels. He explained how the city relied on the solar panels nearly entirely for its operation at a relatively low cost. He provided clear details of their savings on renewable energy.

Her meeting with Mr. Sun provided Energia with a great deal of helpful information. She got the opportunity to hear about some benefits of the solar panels for Sun City. She would learn enthusiastically how the balanced budget of Sun City had a lot to do with their adoption of solar panels. She would understand how the strong economy of the city owed its success to the solar panels.

Mr. Sun and his staff gave Energia a tour of the City Hall. She noticed some sparkly panels covering the roof of the building.

"Why do you have those gleaming plates on top of the roof of the building? What are they for?" she asked teasingly.

"They are our solar panels!" exclaimed Mr. Sun. "The energy they absorb from the sunshine grants power and light to the City Hall. Our office relies on them for efficiency in heating and cooling. We cannot run the City Hall without those panels you see on the rooftop."

Energia could not believe it. She marveled how the sunlight could supply energy so powerfully and so efficiently to that huge building of the City Hall. She would mindfully observe and witness basic facts translating how the City Hall depended utterly on the solar panels for its needs in energy and for a smooth operation daily.

"Wow! They are not joking!" she said to herself in the end. "This is not fake news, it is real; the facts are visible, tangible, and significant here."

The good impression boosted Energia's desire to move on for further observations on the benefits of the solar panels. She would descend on to the streets of Sun City to observe the citizens in the places of their daily activities and interactions, for data collection.

The mayor of Sun City would recommend the members of the Sunny family as key informants for Energia's data collection. In consultation with Energia, he made arrangements with the family to accommodate her during her sojourn in their city.

Initially, Energia had thought of booking a hotel room for her stay in Sun City. But she welcomed the mayor's generous suggestion gladly. Yet, she would quickly reach out to the gatekeeper to understand what the mayor implied by key informants and why she needed them.

"What does Mr. Sun mean by key informants, and what are they for?" she asked Mr. Ethnography shrewdly.

"Key informants," he answered, "are participants or insiders who represent treasured sources of information for your data collection process; they are familiar with the research site and very knowledgeable of the specific information you need for your research. They are valuable assets in ethnography, as they guide the researcher on the field and make participant observation smooth and rewarding. You can trust the key informants the mayor recommends, because they certainly have a good knowledge of Sun City."

After she had left the City Hall, Energia's host family welcomed her warmly into their home. It was a family of four. Mr. and Mrs. Sunny had two daughters. Their names were Sunbird and Sunflower. They lived in a modest house with three bedrooms and three bathrooms. The couple occupied the master bedroom, a large bedroom overlooking a beautiful garden of red roses. Their children stayed in the second bedroom, a medium bedroom facing a peaceful garden of yellow and white roses. The third bedroom was the guestroom, a small bedroom adjacent to an attractive garden of pink roses.

When she walked into the guestroom, Energia noticed only one lamp. This observation shocked her tremendously; she felt that one lamp was not enough for good visibility in a room. In the kingdom of Energium, where she came from, every room had at least three lamps inside, by design. Her parents lived in a big house with five bedrooms, and every room had a minimum of three lamps in.

She would make a similar observation when Sunbird and Sunflower showed her their bedroom, while taking her around the house. She noticed exactly the same thing in the two girls' bedroom, solely a lamp.

She did not understand why there was just one lamp in each bedroom. However, she lacked the courage to ask the sisters about the rationale behind that design.

When came the time for dinner with her host family, there was merely one lamp in the dining room, next to the dining table. Another lamp was in the kitchen. She also perceived only a lamp in the adjacent living room.

After dinner, they all congregated to the family room to spend some time together before bedtime. Energia observed simply one lamp in the family room. In their circle time, Mr. and Mrs. Sunny wondered if Energia had any question for them.

For a split second, Energia thought of seizing that opportunity to ask them why they had only one lamp in each bedroom. At that very moment, she remembered Mr. Chercheur's ethnographic tips on the social decorum, and she withheld her question and controlled her feelings.

Following a brief moment of silence, she smiled and answered, "No, I have no question at this time. Thank you for checking!"

"Are you sure you have no question or comment?" Mrs. Sunny insisted kindly. "Do not be shy! Feel at home."

"I feel blessed to be with your family," Energia answered with a spirited voice, full of emotions. "I am grateful. My first impression is positive. Based upon my first observations, I can tell you are a healthy and happy family. I appreciate your hospitality. Thank you again for welcoming me so kindly!"

After they had left the family room, everybody withdrew quietly in their bedroom. The first night, Energia found it awkward to see and get around with only a lamp. However, by the third night, she felt better. By the end of her stay, she would get used to the dull lamplight; she no longer had any problem seeing around with just a lamp in her room. She would understand that she did not need more than a lamp in her bedroom for enough visibility to read and find her way around.

The lesson was clear as Energia thought of it mindfully: "One lamp is sufficient to see and get around in a room. More than a lamp in a bedroom would reflect greed and result in a waste of energy."

This was a turning point in her life. That meaningful experience and the lesson she learned from it would transform constructively Energia's habits forever upon her return back to Energium.

The next morning, after her first night in the Sunnys' house, Energia did not enjoy a long shower; the water turned cold in the midst of her shower. She would find out that the Sunnys had a small water heater. Their water heater was powered by the solar panels, and they often ran out of hot water. Mrs. Sunny would also inform her that Sun City purposely designed most of its houses with small water tanks and water heaters to prevent its residents from wasting hot water.

Energia could not find in the bathroom any power outlet on the wall to plug in her electric toothbrush and her electric shaving machine. She went to Sunbird and Sunflower for help. The two sisters explained, "Sun City designs the bathrooms of our homes without any electrical outlet on the walls. Our city does not allow electric toothbrushes and electric shaving machines. The residents of Sun City use manual toothbrushes and manual shaving tools."

Sunflower expressly supplied Energia with several packages of manual toothbrushes and a set of manual shaving devices for her stay.

"What about an electric ironing-machine?" Energia asked them. "Do you have any device I could use to press my clothes, like an electric flatiron or a steam iron?"

"Sorry, we do not have any," they told her. "We do not need an ironing machine; we do not iron our clothes here before wearing them."

"How do you remove wrinkles or creases from fabrics or clothing?"

"We make our clothes smooth by rubbing them with our hands!" Sunflower said smiling.

Sunbird would provide a live demonstration of what her sister meant. She spread her skirt on her bed, and rubbed the palms of her hands on it gently, as Energia watched. After spending a few minutes pressing the garment, she asked Energia, "What do you think of the outcome?

"Actually, this is a good idea," she exclaimed, "the result is not bad; your skirt looks nice."

Energia would follow suit. She managed to press her dress with her hands gently and patiently. It took her longer than she had thought. Even though the end result was not as smooth as she would like it to be, the look did not disappoint her.

That morning, she decided to follow Mrs. Sunny to work. Energia's intention was to observe the dynamics of her host mother's workplace. Mrs. Sunny was a nurse, and she worked in a small local health clinic.

As they prepared to leave for the workplace, Mrs. Sunny approached Energia and asked her, "Do know how to ride a bicycle?"

Energia smiled and answered, "Yes, of course, I do."

"That is great!" she exclaimed.

She walked to the backyard and came back with a bicycle for her guest.

Mrs. Sunny grabbed her own bicycle, and Energia followed her, riding behind.

The host mother and her guest were the last two to leave the house on that morning.

Mr. Sunny and her daughters left about one hour earlier. He worked far from home. He was a headmaster. The family had only one car, and it was an electric car. He first had to drop her daughters at their school, before heading to his workplace. He and his daughter usually would leave earlier in the morning for work and for school. Sunbird was a nursing student. Sunflower was in medical school.

As she was riding patiently behind Mrs. Sunny, Energia observed many residents riding bicycles alongside the road. Mrs. Sunny would make her understand that most residents of Sun City owned a bicycle.

"Be aware!" she said. "Hundreds of our residents prefer go to work with bicycles, unless their workplace is too far from home. Some residents select to go on foot if the workplace is within easy walking distance."

Energia observed only a few cars on the road; they all were electric automobiles. Most of the cars in Sun City were electric rechargeable vehicles. Energia did not observe any motorcycle. Mrs. Sunny would explain to her later.

"There are no motorbikes in our city," she said, "they are not allowed here."

"This city," she continued elatedly, "runs only a few city buses for public transportation. Those buses are all electric. Sun City also operates five electric trains around-the-clock. The majority of our residents prefer to use the means of public transportation, because it is free for all the residents of this city. Residents rate our public transportation system highly, because it is very efficient and helpful. My daughters often rely on the public transportation to go to school, whenever their father is unable to drop them."

Upon reaching Mrs. Sunny's workplace, Energia was surprised to notice just two computers on the premises of the health clinic. The computers were for administrative purposes only. They would go from hand to hand, for data entry and data processing. Mrs. Sunny and her coworkers took turns to use them. Energia observed mindfully, as Mrs. Sunny patiently waited for her turn to type and print a patient record for her supervisor.

Unable to make sense of the organizational dynamics here, she whispered in Mrs. Sunny's ear inquisitively, "Why do you have to wait so long, wasting your time around? I suppose this organization is rich, and I do not understand why they would not afford more computers to make your life easy and save time."

"I am not wasting my time, make no mistake about it!" she answered softly. "When I get any information from or on a patient, I write it down with my pen on a piece of paper, and I move on to another case. When the computer becomes available, I record everything on it. It is a lifestyle, our choice. In this clinic, our perception of the time and our approach to our tasks may be different from yours. We do not rush as we care for our patients; filled with compassion for them, we dedicate sufficient time to each patient. We exemplify a philosophy of healthcare that values every patient is worthwhile or time worthy."

Full of admiration, Energia observed Mrs. Sunny spend a whole hour taking care of one patient. "How many patients do you see per day, if I may ask?" she said cautiously.

"In this clinic," Mrs. Sunny replied, "the quantity does not matter; what matters is the quality. We do not perceive patient care through quantitative lenses, but in terms of a qualitative and compassionate dedication. Great patient care requires sufficient time for a kindhearted attention to each patient and a considerate handling of their health issues."

A few moments before five o'clock in the evening, Mrs. Sunny whispered in Energia's ear, "The clinic will close in a few minutes, let us start getting ready for our trip back home."

At five o'clock, the two grabbed their respective bicycle and began their ride back home.

On their way home, Energia asked Mrs. Sunny, "Do you work only day shifts?"

"Yes," she answered, "I work just during the hours of daylight. In Sun City, the sunrise and the sunset regulate our work schedule. The majority of our residents are up and at work at dawn; we go to bed and sleep at dusk. Most businesses would open around seven o'clock in the morning and close around five o'clock in the evening, except for law enforcement, security and safety agencies, the public transportation, hospitals, pharmacies, and other major medical structures."

That answer impressed Energia astonishingly; she was speechless.

Upon arriving home, the guest wanted to wash her dirty laundry.

She asked Mrs. Sunny, "Where is the laundry room, please?"

The host mother took her to a large room with carefully crafted wooden sinks, but with no washer or dryer.

"I cannot see any washer or dryer here. Where are they?" Energia wondered.

"I am sorry, we do not have any of that here, my dear!" Mrs. Sunny replied considerately. "We wash our clothes with our hands, and count on the kindness of the sunshine to dry them outside, in direct sunlight and in the open air."

This answer did not satisfy Energia, she just could not make sense out of it. However, she would not ask any further question, mindful of Mr. Chercheur's research tips. She would understand the absence of an electric washer and dryer simply as another choice in the Sunnys' lifestyle.

The host mother would patiently initiate the guest on how to use her hands to wash clothes. In Energium, Energia had the good reputation of being a fast learner. Yet, learning how to wash her garments with hands was not easy. It would take some time before she could become comfortable. She would get it well eventually. In the end, she was very happy to be able to wash her clothes with hands. There was a time she opened her heart to Mrs. Sunny: "Washing my dresses with hands is actually fun!" she admitted. "It provides a good opportunity for meditation and relaxation."

The next day, she decided to follow Sunbird and Sunflower to their school to continue her observations on the solar panels. The two sisters would seize that opportunity to introduce their guest to the public transportation of Sun City. They made Energia ride on a very comfy electric train to their school. She enjoyed the experience very much to the point that she confided to the two sisters at the end of the ride, "It was quite relaxing. I did not have to worry about any traffic."

Upon arriving in school, the two sisters gave her a tour. They took her to the school cafeteria, library, bookstore, and gymnasium. She observed large solar panels covering the roofs of all the buildings in the school.

In the cafeteria, Energia witnessed students eating with paper plates and wooden forks. She would reveal to the sisters: "This is my first time to see wooden forks. I have never seen them before. I have never imagined or heard of wooden forks before."

"Eating with wooden forks and spoons," they replied, "represents the norm in our school. Everybody eats with wooden forks and spoons here, per the requirements of Sun City. Our city does not allow plastic and metal forks and spoons in the school environment."

"What about the home environment?" she said. "I have noticed you have metal forks and spoons at home; we have been eating with metal forks in your house."

"Good observation!" they exclaimed. "The city allows families to use metal forks and spoons at home, but not plastic forks or spoons. At home, we have the option to use the wooden forks and spoons or the metal ones. Prior to your arrival, our family was using the wooden ones. But on the day when you arrived, our mother stored them and took out the metal forks and spoons to welcome you; she understood you were not used to wooden forks and spoons."

"How kind of her!" Energia shouted with emotions.

When the time came for lunch, the two sisters took her back to the school cafeteria for a treat. She seized that opportunity to try a wooden fork and spoon. It turned out to be a wonderful experience. While they were eating, Energia told the two sisters, "In fact, my wooden fork and spoon are very convenient, easy to use; I wish I had this option in my hometown."

"Do not worry," Sunflower replied, "at the end of your stay, we will pack you a big bag of wooden forks and spoons; we will let you go with sufficient supplies, at least for a year. Hopefully, this will give you enough time to figure out where to acquire them in your hometown."

"If not," Sunbird said, "you are always welcome to order them from Sun City. We will be happy to help ship them over to you. Do not hesitate, feel free to contact us anytime for help."

"I really appreciate your kindness and offer to help!" replied Energia, with a smiley face to express her gratitude.

She would observe a poor luminosity in the cafeteria, in the library, in the bookstore, and in the gymnasium. She made the same observations in the sisters' classrooms. She would not hesitate to complain about it to Sunbird and Sunflower.

The two sisters said, "We do not think the luminosity is low in the buildings of our school. We have enough light to see around. It does not have to be extra bright before we can find our way. Sun City designs its schools with the minimum required amount of light to avoid waste. Our school is powered entirely by the solar panels."

"I am afraid the lack in luminosity might contribute to students ending up blind or with vision problems!" she replied humorously.

But the sisters did not take her answer as a joke.

"Sun City has the lowest rate of blindness in the nation." Sunflower said. "Only a very small number of students wear glasses and contact lenses in our school. Be mindful that an excessive exposure to brightness may also contribute to blindness or poor vision."

"I am sorry," Energia apologized, "bear with me; I promise I will get it; I just need some more time to process and adjust."

"We understand you need some time," Sunbird said, "take your time; there is no rush. It can be difficult for an outsider to understand our practices and the daily life in Sun City."

At the end of the day, Energia was happy to get back on the train with the two sisters. On their ride home, she spent some time observing the general mood on the locomotive. It was a cheerful mood. The passengers felt relaxed, they laughed, and they shared funny stories. It was simply awesome.

She could hardly believe her eyes. It was not like anything she had witnessed in the kingdom of Energium. The observation made her wordless.

The two sisters easily noticed her silence. "Are you fine?" they asked her.

"Yes, I am!" she replied with a smile. "I am just full of admiration for the residents of Sun City; your people are truly happy. In my hometown, at the end of the workday, everybody feels stressed out; most people are grumpy after work; you rarely observe any smile or laugh around you. Meanwhile, here in Sun City, everybody seems to be joyful at the end of the workday; I have the evidence on this ride."

"Every society is different." Sunbird quickly acknowledged.

"I believe people are the products of their cultures." Sunflower added respectfully.

Energia agreed with the sisters and said, "I think your people are the products of a stress-free culture of renewable energies, and my people are the products of a stressful culture of non-renewable energies."

"Honestly speaking, our culture is not stress-free." Sunflower quickly objected. "The culture of renewable energies comes with its own stresses. We simply find constructive ways to address those stresses by being moderate in making choices that are good for us and by making sacrifices in some cases."

Sunbird added, "A happy life requires conscientious choices and sacrifices."

In the wake of that meaningful experience, Energia decided to spend the rest of her time in Sun City riding on the trains. She would travel by train fifty times just to observe the commuters' mood. On each of her ride, she observed happy travelers. They all sang, told funny stories, and giggled, while going to work and while heading back home from work. The passengers' enthusiasm would contaminate Energia eventually. She would join them in singing, laughing, and telling stories to entertain the crowd onboard. The more she got on the trains, the happier she became herself.

The experience impacted her profoundly to the point that she once disclosed to her host mother, "I have observed and experienced on the trains that happiness is contagious."

"We owe that in part to our solar traditions." Mrs. Sunny replied to her. "Allowing the sunrise and the sunset to regulate your life eventually benefits your happiness."

A week later, Energia drew near Sunbird and asked if there was a treadmill in the house. She was dressed up and ready for jogging. The host sister's response would disappoint her.

"In Sun City," Sunbird said graciously, "we do not use treadmills. But we run outdoors, in the open air; we have beautiful parks, carefully designed for jogging, nature bath, or forest bathing."

"Would you mind taking me to the nearest park for jogging?" Energia asked courteously.

Sunbird gladly accepted, got ready, and went to the nearest park with her guest.

The wonderful scene Energia contemplated in park mesmerized her. She saw some residents jogging; others were enjoying forest bathing. A small number of residents were meditating.

"It seems everybody is fit here!" she said to her host sister.

"That is a huge compliment to our city," Sunbird replied with excitement. "I appreciate it; most of our residents find time to exercise daily."

As they both kept on jogging, the host sister went faster than her guest.

"You are as strong as a horse!" Energia said to her.

"No!" Sunbird replied, while giggling. "I do not want to be as strong as a horse; I am not a horse, obviously."

Energia first laughed, then she said, "That is an idiomatic way of saying you are physically fit."

But the host sister insisted, "I want to be as strong as a human being, I am a human being not a horse."

"I am deeply sorry," Energia apologized, "I did not mean to offend you."

"In Sun City," Sunbird said, "we tend to avoid certain metaphors and hyperboles that stress the human nature, by comparing the human beings to others animals. We want to value the humankind and recognize its strengths, but also its limitations. Evidently, a human being cannot be as strong as a horse."

"I fully respect your view, it makes sense!" Energia said humbly. "Maybe, some comparisons actually alienate the human beings and push them beyond their natural potentials."

"That is fair enough," Sunbird agreed. "Thank you for understanding what I mean!"

Toward the end of her time in Sun City, Energia's host family took her to a mega concert in town. It was on a Saturday at two o'clock in the afternoon. She observed the scarcity of light in the concert hall. On the main stage, there was just enough light for the audience to identify the singers' faces. There was no extraordinary display of fancy or colorful lights, like what you would see in the Kingdom of Energium under the same circumstances. Yet, the concert went very well to the satisfaction of the public. Energia really enjoyed it. She would use that venue to show her host family her dancing skills. Energia was a great dancer. Her dancing moves impressed Mr. and Mrs. Sunny; they earned her a standing ovation from Sunbird and Sunflower.

After thirty days, Energia's adventures in Sun City came to an end. She had conducted a total of seventy observations across Sun City. Thirty-five of her observations had lasted only one hour each, five observations had covered only two hours each, and thirty participant-observations were for eight hours each. The locations of observations were very diverse and multiform; they included the City Hall, the Sunnys' house, different organizations (including medical centers and schools), the streets, the public transportation, the marketplaces, and a concert hall.

Initially, Chercheur had advised Energia to spend up to three months in Sun City for reliability and validity in data collection. He had said to Energia, "Ideally, ethnography would require a few months of prolonged and in-depth participant-observations. The technique of participant-observation requires that you immerse yourself in a culture and become like an insider. You would spend up to three or six months to understand the cultural patterns with a hands-on experience on the site for representative data and for reliable and valid outcome."

But after spending a month in Sun City, Energia wrapped it up; she made up her mind that she had completed enough observations and obtained sufficient data to move on to the next step in the process of her research.

Following her successful experience in Sun City with Mr. Ethnography's golden advice, Energia deeply understood the importance of having a research advisor in every research process. She resolved she would often seek some guidance from her advisor at every stage of her research for success. From that moment, she would settle and travel with Mr. Chercheur, and she resorted to his expertise and services at every step of the process of her research.

From Sun City, she headed to the second major stop in her process of data collection, another city called Wind City, to continue her research on renewable energy. She embarked on that journey with her research advisor, Mr. Chercheur.

CHAPTER 3

Energia's Qualitative Interviews

Wind City is a costal township with good speed winds throughout the calendar year. On their way to that city, Energia and Chercheur drove through green valleys and hills, on a stretch of curvy road with sharp inclines and steep declines, with road signs indicating that the road climbed at a gradient of six percent, a slope implying that the road gained six feet in elevation for every one hundred feet of horizontal distance. They travelled across a number of beautiful and immense parks, varying in size; they were wind parks or wind farms used to generate electricity. Some of those wind power plants hosted about ten wind turbines, while others carried up to a hundred wind turbines or wind energy converters.

Impressed by the majestic movement of the turbines, those large structures with spinning blades, Energia stopped to take some time to contemplate them peacefully. Chercheur would explain that the blades were connected to electro-magnetic generators that produced electricity whenever the wind triggered the blades to spin. Energia and Chercheur would not understand how vital such wind power stations were to life in Wind City until their arrival at the city hall, and during their first meeting with the mayor of Wind City, Mr. Wind.

Mr. Wind welcomed Energia and Chercheur warmly in his commodious office. They spent some time chatting on the goal of their visit. The mayor praised Energia's interest in Wind City.

"We greatly appreciate your interest in our city; your visit honors our citizens tremendously," he said graciously.

In a symbolic gesture, he handed a key of the city to Energia and Chercheur to allow them to unlock every door and to have access to every household and office in Wind City for data collection.

Mr. Wind would entertain Energia on how he supplied his city with the wind all year round to meet the citizens' needs in renewable energy. He would boast about the large wind power stations his city put in place for mechanical power or electricity.

He said, "Here, our main energy source is reliable environmentally; it is safe and low-cost. The wind farms produced a record fifty-five percent of electricity in Wind City last year; wind energy accounted for more than a hundred terawatt-hours."

He gladly unveiled to his guests the budget of Wind City on wind power plants. He explained how the city relied on the wind farms nearly entirely for its operation, at a relatively low cost. He provided clear details of their savings on wind energy.

"We had traveled across some wind parks on our way here," Energia said with a smile.

"You had only seen a few," Mr. Wind replied, "we have more, small and large onshore and offshore wind farms. Wind City benefits from a large offshore wind plant located on the beautiful river running by our city."

Their meeting with Mr. Wind provided Energia with a great deal of helpful information. She got the opportunity to hear about some benefits of the wind power for Wind City. She would learn enthusiastically how the balanced budget of Wind City had a lot to do with their adoption of wind energy. She would understand how the strong economy of the city owned its success to the wind farms.

Mr. Wind and his staff gave Energia and Chercheur a tour of the city hall. On the tour, Energia and Chercheur got some good taste of the magnitude of what wind energy could achieve. Mr. Wind's relaxed demeanor and his colleagues' enthusiasm also made a positive impact. On the tour, Mr. Wind surprised Energia and Chercheur with the news that the city would welcome them officially in the setting of a town hall meeting, immediately after the tour.

Energia was not sure how to respond, and she looked at Chercheur suspiciously.

Chercheur smiled and said quickly, "That is awesome, we feel honored. Thank you!"

Energia understood immediately, and she added, "We welcome and appreciate your offer greatly. We look forward to that town forum with excitement."

As Mr. Wind and his staff withdrew for a few minutes to check on the crowd of citizens showing up for the welcome ceremony, Chercheur whispered to Energia, "This is a great opportunity for interviewing the citizens over their experiences of wind energy."

"That sounds great," she replied, "but how are we going to do this? I did not prepare for this activity."

"Listen, young lady," he said, "an interview is simply a qualitative method for attaining knowledge by asking your interviewees open-ended questions in a data collection process."

"I know that, Sir! But I have not written down any questions!" she exclaimed.

"Do not worry," he reassured her, "you just ask them any question that crosses your mind. We call it unstructured interview. Remember we are here to conduct interviews for a qualitative case-study and a phenomenology of the benefits of wind energy in Wind City"

"What do you mean by unstructured interview?" she asked.

"An unstructured interview process," he answered, "refers to a qualitative data collection technique where you ask the participants randomly any open-ended questions that come to your mind, and in the order they come. You do not have to write down your questions beforehand. Such things as the contexts or cultures, the parties and their personalities, and recent events or current issues could trigger your questions. Be reassured, I stand by you, right here, to assist you anytime you need help in the daunting process. You can count on me, I mean what I say."

"I appreciate your assistance," she pointed out, with mixed emotions. "It is certainly reassuring, and the explanation you provide is eye-opening. However, I still need some clarification on what you mean by a case-study and a phenomenology."

"In a research process," he remarked, "when you undertake interviews that focus on a single case, such as an event, an intervention, a person, a group, a community, neighborhood, a city, an organization, a nation, or any other single entity or unit of analysis, that strategy goes by the name of a qualitative case study. A qualitative case study could also encompass a small number of cases varying is size from two to ten."

"However," he continued, "in the process of your study, when your interviews emphasize the participants' experiences of an event, an intervention, an issue, a job, a culture, or anything relating to their lives, we call it phenomenology, which is also a qualitative research strategy."

"What about a unit of analysis?" Energia wondered, while tipping her hand. "I am interested in that, please tell me about it."

"A unit of analysis," he answered softly, "is the entity your analysis focuses on for data collection and analysis in the research process; depending of the emphasis of a study, the unit of analysis could be individuals, groups, cities, nations, events, books, journals, magazines, websites, newspapers, articles, pictures, songs, conflicts, mediations, peacekeeping operations, test scores, universities, schools, organizations, businesses, or others. You could perceive the unit of analysis as the '*who*' or the '*what*' of your analysis. In the case of your study, the unit of analysis could be *energy sources* or *energy types*; it could also be *cities*."

Before Energia could thank Chercheur for clarifying the concepts, Mr. Wind reemerged suddenly and invited his two visitors to follow him to the podium in the great hall for the town forum.

As they entered the hall, Energia and Chercheur could not believe their eyes; citizens of all ages packed the great hall. According Chercheur's estimates, there were more than one hundred people in the hall.

Mr. Wind would confirm there were exactly one hundred and ten citizens in the hall.

Energia could not help but say, "Your citizens are very nice and welcoming."

Mr. Wind replied, "It is our tradition in Wind City, it is our practice."

At the sight of the large size of the crowd, Chercheur apprised her to Energia, "We may need to conduct a focus group interview."

She did not understand what he meant, but she nodded to agree with him, without thinking.

Mr. Wind moved onto the podium to introduce Energia and Chercheur solemnly.

The crowd stood up and welcomed them with a round of applause, it was loud and sustained.

Following the standing ovation from the audience, the mayor advised his citizens to sit down, and he allowed the two guests to the podium to speak to the crowd.

In a very polite and tactful manner, Energia unveiled the purpose of their visit to Wind City.

The audience got sold to the idea. After the crowd had welcomed the plan, Mr. Wind helped pass the informed consent forms around, while Energia withdrew with Chercheur to a remote corner of the room to ponder the modalities of how to tailor the process.

"I feel we are in trouble," she said anxiously. "How do we go with interviewing more than more hundred people?"

"Do not worry," he reassured. "We will go by focus groups?"

"What do you mean by focus groups?" she asked.

"Focus groups," he replied, "would allow us to break down the large group randomly into smaller groups. We would interview the smaller groups instead of each individual in the large group."

"How do we do that in practice?" she persisted.

"We have one hundred and ten citizens," he answered. "We could divide them into eleven groups of ten people, and we would interview the eleven groups instead of one hundred and ten individuals."

"Can you provide more specifics about the process of that type of interview?" she went on.

Before Chercheur could answer that question, Mr. Wind approached Energia and whispered that the audience was excited and ready for the interview.

Mindful of Energia's question, Chercheur took the lead and randomly divided the participants into eleven groups of ten people.

After thanking the participants for willing to participate in the research, Chercheur would carefully explain the purpose of the focus group interviews and provide details about the process.

He said, "Per the informed consent form you have signed, the purpose of these interviews is to explore the benefits of wind energy for the citizens of Wind City. We encourage you to discuss with your groupmates over the advantages of wind energy, based on your own experiences. At the start of your discussions, each group will select a member to moderate its discussions and facilitate the group dynamics. In terms of the ground rules, we will silence our phones and listen to others as we patiently wait for our turn to talk. Ms. Energia and I will coordinate the discussions for all eleven groups by moving from one group to another one. Per the informed consent form, we will tape-record the discussions."

"Would you mind telling our citizens what the results of your research will be for?" Mr. Wind asked up front.

"Interesting point!" Energia exclaimed. "Per the informed consent form, we will analyze the data collected and publish the results for policymaking on renewable energy. For confidentiality, we will not mention any personal names in the publication."

Mrs. Weather, a renowned citizen of Wind City, asked promptly, "What are the specific tasks of the moderator in each group?"

"The moderator's tasks," said Chercheur, "include opening the discussion session by welcoming the groupmates cordially and respectfully, presenting the discussion question formally to the group, empowering the members for active participation in the discussions, enforcing the ground rules, and recording the discussions. The moderator is also a timekeeper. The success of a group depends, to a large extent, on the moderator's humble leadership."

Mr. Case Study, a senior citizen of Wind City, asked eagerly, "Do we speak solely based upon our experience living in Wind City, or can we factor into the equation our experiences in some other parts of the world we had lived in?"

"Great question!" answered Energia devotedly. "We are doing a case study of Wind City, we are interested only in your life experience in Wind City at this point."

Mrs. Phenomenology, Mr. Case Study's sister, followed suit and asked keenly, "How long is a focus group interview?"

Through some rapid and telling eye contacts, Chercheur and Energia spent a few seconds checking with Mr. Wind before answering.

"We plan to spend the next two hours together," said Chercheur. "But it depends on the groups and their needs. Some groups could finish early, while others would take longer."

"There is no rush," Energia added serenely, "it is important that each group observes its pace for everyone to feel comfortable in the process. We thank you again for taking the time to join us for this amazing research experience."

While Energia continued to speak to the large audience, Chercheur called on Mr. Wind and a few participants to help arrange the discussion settings. They organized the chairs in eleven circles of ten chairs. Five groups of ten people would fit inside the hall and six groups of ten people outside under graceful acacia trees.

Chercheur rejoined the audience and assigned each group to its location for the proceedings of the focus group interviews.

Both Energia and Chercheur toured the eleven groups actively and engaged with their members respectfully, as the participants discussed the benefits of wind energy and shared their experiences pertaining to Wind City. The proceedings unfolded smoothly under their watch. The focus groups turned out to be successful in collecting reliable data on benefits of wind energy for the citizens of Wind City.

In light of this success story and the quality of the data they collected, Energia confided to Chercheur, "Certainly, focus group interviews provide effective techniques for qualitative data collection."

Chercheur would advise Energia to follow up with semi-structured and structured interviews using purposeful sampling.

To heed his advice, she would seize the opportunity of the focus groups to recruit some participants purposefully for follow-up semi-structured and structured interviews. She went around each of the eleven focus groups, asking for participants to volunteer for follow-up semi-structured or structured interviews. A total of fifty participants accepted her invitation by volunteering to participate in follow-up semi-structured or structured interviews the next day. The volunteers included Mr. Wind and his sister

Breeze, Mrs. Weather, Mr. Biography, Ms. Rain, Mrs. Phenomenology and her brother Case Study.

With Chercheur's assistance, Energia spent her night working on specific qualitative questions for the structured interviews. She wrote down a series of open-ended interview questions, including the following:

"What are your opinions on wind energy?"

"What do you think are some benefits of wind energy to the environment in Wind City?"

"How do you think the use of wind energy contributes to lowering air pollution and carbon dioxide emissions in Wind City?"

"In what ways do you think wind energy minimizes the rate of global warming and climate change?"

"How do you compare wind energy and hydrocarbon fuels?"

"Feel free to discuss any related issue you would like to bring up."

In the process of the one-on-one structured interviews, Energia asked each of the fifty participants the same set of questions. As each participant answered the questions, Energia and Chercheur listened carefully, and they recorded the answers with the consent of each respondent.

In their responses, Mr. Wind, Ms. Breeze, Mr. Biography, Mrs. Weather, Ms. Rain, Mrs. Phenomenology, and Mr. Case Study credited the use of wind energy for rare or extremely low greenhouse gas emissions for an overall good environment in Wind City.

Mrs. Phenomenology said excitedly, "By vocation, I study life experiences, what the human beings say or share about the different things they experience in the time and space of existence for meaning-making. My answer would reflect and value our people's experiences with wind energy. Per our citizens' experiences and per my own life experience in Wind City, we breathe healthy air and drink clean water here. This is because our wind plants do not emit any pollutant into our water or air."

Mr. Case Study concurred elatedly, "What I do in life is to examine in depth an object, a situation, an event, a person, a group, or any other entity over a period of time for understanding social reality. Evidence shows lower total air pollution and carbon dioxide emissions in the case of Wind City in comparison to other neighboring cities that generate their electricity from fossil fuels."

Mr. Wind followed suit and said, "We are grateful for our geographic location, it suits well the promotion of wind energy. Per a recent study by our valued citizen, Case Study, the total offshore and onshore wind energy potential in Wind City is estimated at over 150 gigawatts (GW), which is higher than what neighboring cities experience. Mindful of that fact, our city council and policymakers design appropriate legislations and take relevant actions to tailor policymaking to our great asset in wind. Citizens from all strata, local businesses, and city officials eagerly commit to make wind energy a successful industry in Wind City. The wind energy is a source of pride for our city. It stimulates our economic growth; the sector of wind energy famously employs over four thousand citizens. Local businesses work tirelessly to back city leaders' efforts in promoting the use of wind energy; they support our noble common cause, by providing meaningful incentives and tangible rewards to galvanize and empower every citizen that relies on wind energy. I give credit to the good will of our citizens; they abide by the city rules and participate in the process actively, regardless of their political affiliations. Their compliance with the city regulations makes success easier to achieve. Success is obvious when everybody is on board with a good political will. Offshore and onshore wind energy largely contributes to the energy security of Wind City, and this ultimately allows us to counter climate change effectively."

Ms. Breeze joined the conversation and said softly, "I had spent five years of my life working in the kingdom of Energium. They were the worst five years of my life, all things considered. During those years, I had experienced chronic headaches or severe migraines constantly, I was depressed and scared for my health. My doctors tried to help as much as they could. Eventually, I moved from Energium ten years ago and relocated to Wind City per my primary doctor's recommendation.

"After moving here," she continued wisely, "my headaches suddenly vanished, I felt relaxed, and I experienced positive energy around the clock. Per my experience, the use of wind energy presents socio-environmental and economic advantages. The socio-environmental benefits are quite obvious, in terms of low CO_2 emissions; I breathe clean air in Wind City compared to the highly polluted air my lungs used to inhale in Energium. I feel healthier. Here, I also save a lot of money on energy in comparison to how much I had spent in Energium. My math finds that I now spend three times less than what I was spending in the kingdom of Energium on electric bills."

Mr. Biography jumped in to present some data.

"By profession," he said enthusiastically, "I interview random or nonrandom samples of human subjects to provide qualitative written accounts of human lives. My answer here presents briefly a cost-benefit analysis of the turbines in Wind City from the perspectives of a random sample of citizens I have interviewed on the topic of our discussion. Citizens report that the spinning blades of the turbines can be noisy; the blades also strike flying birds at times. But the citizens in the sample feel happy with wind energy; they find it affordable and healthy."

Mrs. Weather jumped right in and said, "Offshore and onshore wind is abundant and available in our city all year round. The profusion of wind as our primary resource and commodity is a strategic blessing, and we work hard and strategically to take advantage of it to the benefit of our physical, mental, and environmental health. Per the results of recent interviews that our city radio and the weather channel conducted on the streets of Wind City, wind energy accounts for more than ninety percent in keeping our citizens healthy, per the views of one hundred citizens randomly selected and interviewed. That is significant for policymaking."

Ms. Rain adopted a unique approach. She would address Energia's questions and concerns, while discussing other related issues, based on her travel experiences.

"We are lucky in Wind City!" she exclaimed. "The type of wind we enjoy here is kind, we need to take advantage of it fully. It is not always the case elsewhere, the wind can get very nasty and damaging nowadays. I witnessed that type of destructive wind recently, during my vacation in a country called Ogabot. Ogabot is a beautiful series of small islands. During my sojourn, a high wind hit a minor coastal city of Ogabot in the midst of a heavy rain pouring down. The wind blew hard and knocked down everything on its way. It flattened most of the houses and buildings in the city. The heavy rain did not help the situation in any way; the rivers flooded over the city, and it collapsed completely. The wind and the floods wiped the entire city off the map. It was a terrible environmental disaster in Ogabot. In my opinion that tragedy provides a reminder that the human excessive use of the fossil fuels could contribute to making the wind and the rain go crazy as in Ogabot. In addition to that disaster, I also witnessed dangerous rises in sea levels threatening the very existence of the islands of Ogabot. I visited a small island disappearing slowly under unexpectedly invasive seawaters. Let's beware and behave here and now, my people!"

Energia patiently interviewed all fifty participants, one by one. She listened deeply to each one of them with interest. With the consent of each participant, she wrote down notes and recorded some interviews. In the end, she was happy with the data she collected from the interviews and what she learned on the benefits of wind energy in Wind City. She thought the experience was rewarding.

The process and outcome of the structured interviews encouraged Energia to network with the participants for follow-up semi-structured interviews. Forty-five of the same interviewees agreed to follow up with semi-structured interviews. She got their telephone contacts and email addresses for the follow-up interviews. The next day, she called some of the participants on the phone and reached out to others by emails with more or less personalized questions for semi-structured interviews.

Ms. Rain was one of the participants who joined Energia for the follow-up. She was eager to talk freely about her recent visit to a country called Acirfa.

"I was recently in Acirfa," she said, "to console and help a group of farmers. They have been crying for some rain for so long. They had spent nearly twelve months without any raindrop. Due to the lack of rain, they had no crop, and their cattle died. Even xerophilous animals and plants in the region succumbed; some of the brave donkeys and camels used for farming activities died of thirst, and the cactus plants dried up. The farmers and their community suffered drought and famine. I visited them in their farms and several other local sites, to reward them with some water. They were happy to welcome me in their land. They took me to the symbolic site of a drying river, the only remaining water reserve in their community, and it was preserved strictly for human consumption. What used to be a healthy green valley lost its greenery completely; even the evergreen plants on the shoreline gave up their natural color. It was a scary scene to witness. This reminded me that our aggressive use of non-renewable energy could contribute to a lack of rain in some regions of the world; some parts of the globe are more vulnerable than others, as they suffer the effects of human-made environmental disasters more drastically."

In her design of the semi-structured interviews, Energia included some standard questions for all the respondents. But she tailored other questions to each individual respondent's needs, depending on their identity, their age, their gender, their lifestyle, their income, and their personal experience of relying on wind energy. On the phone, she would ask the participants additional questions alongside the written one, based on the respondent's personality, needs, and context of life.

To her satisfaction, the data she collected from the semi-structured interviews validated the findings of the structured interviews, in terms of the benefits of wind energy for the citizens of Wind City.

Soon afterward, she hurried off to her advisor to express some excitement about the results.

After celebrating the findings with her, Chercheur spoke up. "Remember," he said, "research is like light; it illuminates the researcher and society on reality. Conducting research is like lighting a lamp and putting it on a lampstand, where it gives light for society to discover some hidden aspects of reality for constructive changes."

"I appreciate that you inform me of your discoveries, they are precious." he continued didactically. "You will also need to find ways to spread the word to society at large; every scientific discovery is a treasure for social learning and behavioral improvement. Be mindful that the dissemination of the information will come as the crowning of your research process, to make the outcomes useful to society."

"What a meaningful metaphor!" exclaimed Energia. "You seem to provide here a transparent and pertinent definition of what research is and does."

"I am glad you understand this so quickly and clearly," he replied happily. "You just need to remember that the overall research process requires repetitions, recommencements, and the researcher's perpetual recommitments as a result. Please do not give up in the midst of the challenges, they are inherent to the process. If you carry on the research activities mindfully and hold out to the end, you will not be disappointed, useful outcomes will reward you satisfactorily."

As the end of their time in Wind City drew near, the two fellows seized the opportunity of the final days to attend a well-anticipated international conference on climate change in Wind City. Both the theme and venue of the climate conference were timely, it all coincided nicely with Energia's data collection period in the city. There could not be a better opportunity in this case, no wonder Energia made up her mind to participate in the proceedings.

The conference gathered many world leaders and climate activists from around the globe. They came together to discuss and advocate for creative and speedy ways to promote renewable energy sources and curb carbon emissions, for the sake of environmental and public health.

The meeting set out to bring a sense of urgency, by pushing world leaders to no longer be complacent over climate change and global warming. The talks and presentations aggressively set the tempo of the conference and maintained the sense of urgency; they presented the dire conditions facing our environments and called out policymakers to act sooner than later. As Chercheur put it in his presentation, "the trends show clearly and significantly that the existence of the earth (with all species living on it) is in serious jeopardy."

"This is no joke, the evidence is compelling, my friends!" he went on, while painting a black picture of global warming and climate change to his audience. "Mother Earth is on the brink of collapse! With rising temperatures, our planet is cooking fast on the highly heated stove of our greedy choices. Ironically, we are the stubborn and horrible cooks, for we burn the earthy menu stupidly with our immoderate usage of the fossil fuels. Our excessive consumption of hydrocarbon energy is a misfortune for climate sustainability, and it presents a grim threat to public and environmental health. We cannot afford to practice carpe diem with regard to non-renewable energy, we need to be mindful of the future of the earth. We all need to act to counter the current trends; if we can take action *hic et nunc*, so much the better."

Ms. Snow, the youngest conferee, would interrupt Chercheur with what she considered to be a burning question. "Please, sir!" she pleaded passionately. "Would you tell me more about it?"

"Certainly, young lady! I am all ears, we need to listen to the youth, proceed with your question!" he answered eagerly.

"What shall we compare non-renewable and renewable energy sources to?" she asked inquisitively.

She was a fresh and spirited climate activist, and she used her presentation at the conference to urge global leaders on the need to curb emissions of greenhouse gases drastically and immediately.

Chercheur had found her question so appealing that he reframed it for himself, before he could think of an answer.

"What shall we say the non-renewable energy sources are like?" he asked, perplexed.

"What analogy shall we use to explain renewable energy sources?" he persisted.

He paused and closed his eyes for a while to think of an emblematic and didactic response.

As soon as he got a clear answer, he opened his eyes widely. "Eureka!" he cried loudly.

"I got it for you," he continued with a smile. "To some extent, the non-renewable energy sources are like wells built on a putrefying lake that pollutes its environment and ends up drying out. Meanwhile, renewable energy sources are like wells built on a regenerating river that rejuvenates its environment and never dries up."

The audience instantly rose to the occasion to welcome his response outstandingly, with a standing ovation. The spontaneous positive reaction from the crowd clearly illustrated they were satisfied beyond their expectations.

Ms. Snow delightfully expressed her feelings of full satisfaction. "What an eloquent analogy!" she exclaimed. "I could not expect a better answer."

Energia enjoyed the interactions. She admired the political good will of many climate activists and researchers working tirelessly to redeem the earth from the big mess of global warming. She managed to network effectively with many of them. But she also expressed her frustration at the political leaders who lacked good will or those still in denial of the human factors contributing to climate change. She used her presentation to send them a vehement message, calling on them to have the courage to look at the evidence mindfully and honestly.

"The facts are actual and irresistible, they speak loudly to all of us, and they beg for attention," she said pitifully, while staring at a few political leaders and pleading to save the planet.

After multiple deliberations, the conference resulted in a stream of resolutions for curbing carbon emissions and promoting renewable energy. Energia had doubts about the sincerity of some political leaders in working for the implementation of the key decisions reached at the conference, but she highly valued the conclusions of the international gathering. She thought of the meeting as a good initiative and a foremost encouraging step toward collaborative problem-solving. She praised the positive act in the fact that world leaders and climate activists and researchers were able to meet and have a constructive dialogue on dire climate issues. She evaluated the meeting as a major step forward.

"Each footstep in the right direction is significant," she said. "Even every small step brings us closer to the desired goal."

Chercheur would confirm her uncertainties when he came up close to Energia to cast doubt on the implementation of specific conclusions. "This may be embarrassing, but let us be realistic," he said nervously, while holding the comprehensive list of resolutions in his hands. "The gap between these decisions and their implementation remains huge and deep; we can only hope and pray for charismatic leadership with good political will for the implementation."

Energia appreciated his mentor's honesty, but she wanted to get to understand his motivations. "Why are you so pessimistic over this?" she asked adamantly.

"There are real and rigid political divides that would impair the implementation of some decisions," he answered sensitively.

"Do you mean some of these resolutions are unrealistic?" she persisted.

"Not at all! Actually, they all are realistic decisions," he argued. "However, we cannot ignore the drama of partisan politics in notable countries; it is real and damaging to constructive social change and progressive policymaking on climate issues."

The gathering provided a great venue to recognize and empower climate activists and researchers, many of whom received incentives and rewards. Energia was happily surprised to find herself among the laureates.

Chercheur had nominated her, without telling her. She was pleased to be recognized for her research. She got a substantial financial award for her initiative to conduct research on renewable energy. She was extremely grateful to her advisor for the nomination.

CHAPTER 4

Energia's Quantitative Experiments and Surveys

U pon her return to Energium for a break, after three months of absence, Energia organized a big party to celebrate her return. She invited her former classmates in high school and college. The event turned out to be a big gathering with fifty-five of her friends. At the party, the guests were excited to listen to the host share her research adventures. Energia skillfully used the opportunity to inform them about her upcoming departure for a vacation in a strategic location called Choice City, another coastal city next to Energium.

Mr. Experiment, a famous research strategist, had developed Choice City as an environment for experimenting how the use of renewable energy could affect the human beings in their choice of activities and health, in comparison to their use of non-renewable energy. It turned out to be a popular destination for vacation. Choice City was on the pathway of a major river crossing the region. The city was the site of a powerful hydraulic barrage used to generate electricity for its citizens. Choice City was renowned for running on both renewable energy and non-renewable energy sources. The city gave its residents and neighborhoods the freedom to choose consistently between hydraulic energy and energy generated from the fossil fuels.

Energia would seize the opportunity of the party to announce that she would pay fully for the stay of any friend who was willing to join her for an experiment in Choice City during her vacation.

"I may be willing to join, if you are willing to explain what you mean by experiment," interrupted Ms. Heat, one of her closest friends.

Chercheur was in attendance, and he stepped up to meet the challenge.

"An experiment," he said, "is a scientific method for understanding reality and obtaining knowledge through testing and comparing."

"Thank you, sir, for the definition!" Ms. Heat exclaimed. "It is helpful, I am all in, and I am definitely for it."

"But aren't there different types of experiments?" asked Kabi, another guest in attendance. "Would you mind clarifying the different types of experiments for our information?"

"I am glad to do it," replied Chercheur. "My typology of experiments would classify them into two major rubrics. The first rubric would encompass any experiment conducted with a control group; the second rubric would include any experiment performed without a control group."

"What are some characteristics of each grouping? Be more specific, sir!" Kabi said.

"Please tell us amply about each category," Ms. Heat beseeched Chercheur.

"The process of any experiment in the first rubric would require a control group and a treatment group," Chercheur replied. "The treatment group is the one receiving the treatment or intervention in an experimental design; you can also call it the study group. The control group is the standard group to which the experimenter compares the treatment group. In the event of a random assignment of cases from the control group to the treatment group, we call the procedure a random assignment experiment or a classical experiment. In the absence of a random assignment of cases, we call it a nonrandom assignment experiment."

"What should we understand by a random assignment?" Ms. Heat asked.

"A random assignment," Chercheur answered, "occurs when the experimenter randomly assigns a number of cases from the control group to the treatment group in the process of an experiment."

"Some illustrations would help us tremendously," suggested Kedu, a well-informed guest in attendance.

"Suppose I bring two large identical cages C1 and C2 alongside a liquid product P," Chercheur replied. "The cages were made with the same materials, by the same artisan, on the same day, at the same time, and in the same context. Their internal environments and conditions are exactly the same. The first cage C1 has twenty healthy mice inside, and the second cage C2 is empty. All twenty mice were born on the same day, at the same time, in the same year, and from the same genetrix. They have everything in common and share the same phenotypes. They were all raised in the same farm and fed similarly. Right here, in your presence, I randomly assign ten mice from the first cage C1 to the second cage C2. At this point the mice in both cages keep jumping happily. Then, I decide to inject the liquid product P to the mice in the second cage C2. Each mouse in cage C2 receives the same dose of P and starts sleeping immediately afterward. Meanwhile the mice in cage C1 keep jumping without exception. I will conclude that P is a sleeping pill."

"If I understand correctly, C1 hosts the control group and C2 the treatment group," Energia interrupted.

"Well done! You got it!" Chercheur confirmed.

"I think the random assignment in this case occurs when you randomly assign ten mice from C1 to C2. Is that correct?" Kabi wondered.

"You have nailed it down. Good job!" Chercheur declared.

"This is obviously a classical experiment, because we have a control group, a treatment group, and a random assignment," Ms. Heat stated.

"That is correct. Congratulations!" Chercheur exclaimed.

"Not so fast!" Ms. Heat reacted. "I continue to struggle with understanding the notion of random assignment."

"What is the difference between a random selection and a random assignment?" she asked.

"Your concern is fair, and your question relevant," Chercheur acknowledged. "A random selection happens at the very beginning of a study, when the researcher selects a subset of a larger population for study, by giving everyone an equal chance of being selected to partake in the study. The random assignment occurs later in the process of the study, when the researcher assigns randomly a number of cases from a previously selected sample to a treatment or study group. In short, the random selection is from a population, whereas the random assignment is from a sample."

"I am grateful to you for a very helpful explanation, sir!" Ms. Heat said.

"How about the second rubric of your typology?" Kabi asked politely.

"Every experiment in the second rubric intervenes on a single group, as in a logic of pretest and posttest," Chercheur affirmed. "For instance, when a study compares how a group of subjects deals with personal conflicts before their exposure to meditation and how they handle conflicts after practicing meditation. This form of experiment has no control group; it does not involve any random assignment. You could call it a single group experiment."

Awestruck by Chercheur's intelligible responses, Sanjo, another voice in attendance, would ask him out of curiosity, "Any additional words for us on the role of the research hypothesis in an experiment?"

"The hypothesis," Chercheur explained, "is actually the general opinion (the affirmative or negative tentative answer to your research question) that your experiment or study will test in an attempt to confirm it or reject it. Its structure reflects the relationship or the lack of relationship between the independent variable and the dependent variable. The independent variable is the predicting variable; you could also call it the grouping variable or the predictor. The dependent variable is the outcome variable or the predicted variable, it depends on the independent variable; you can also call it the test variable."

Energia was grateful to her advisor for clarifying the concepts so meaningfully; he solved the puzzle wisely and satisfactorily. She gave every guest an equal chance to be selected for the vacation. At the news, some friends offered spontaneously to join her for the vacation in Choice City. She handed each volunteer an informed consent form explaining the purpose and procedures of the experiment. The purpose of the experiment would be to confirm or reject the research hypothesis that the type of energy source the participants relied on would affect their lifestyle and health. A random group of twenty guests signed the consent forms to formalize their intention to participate in the experiment.

A week later, Energia and her twenty friends traveled to two famous resorts in Choice City. The twenty friends had the same living standards, they were of the same age, and shared the same spending habits. After reaching Choice City, Energia randomly assigned ten friends (the treatment or study group) to spend the month of vacation in a resort that ran one hundred percent on hydraulic energy. Meanwhile, the other ten friends (the control group) would spend the same month in a similar resort that ran one hundred percent on the fossil fuels.

Mr. Experiment owned and ran the two resorts. He was accredited and respected for his high sense of fair play. He had designed the two resorts carefully, and his team had built them to be identical to some degree. The houses in the two resorts had the same dimensions, they were designed and built by the same builders with identical materials. However, the two resorts carried different names; they were located in two different neighborhoods. Mr. Experiment called first resort by the name of *Renewable Energy Resort* (RER), and the second one was the *Non-Renewable Energy Resort* (NRER). The RER was in a neighborhood that ran on hydropower, also known as water power, and the NRER was in a neighborhood that ran on the fossil fuels. The two resorts were about fifteen miles apart.

At the end of the month, the friends in the treatment group (the RER group) reported a lower spending on electricity. The monthly amount spent on electricity for the control group was three times higher than the one for the study group. Individuals in the treatment group also reported lower stress levels compared to those in the control group. At the end of the month, the systolic blood pressure, the pulse pressure, and the mean arterial blood pressure were significantly lower for the individuals in the RER treatment group in comparison to those in the NRER control group. At the end of the month, the experiment recorded a higher mean in the blood pressures of the individuals in the NRER control group, when compared with the mean of the blood pressures of those in the RER test group.

The study group reported they had spent more time sleeping, walking in natural gardens, playing social games together, and telling funny stories, than watching TV or spending time on the phone or on the computer. They had slept at least eight hours every night, and they had taken a nap for at least one hour every day. Due to the fact its neighborhood operated on hydroelectric power, and mindful of saving energy, the RER group put in place a number of policies for regulating their energy use, by promoting what they called a rational and moderate usage of energy. Such policies would not allow any activity or game involving heavy machinery (such as the roller coasters) on the premises of the RER or its immediate vicinity; they would not tolerate cars and motorcycles in and around the RER. They only permitted bicycling and walking in their beautiful gardens. They would promote swimming activities and circle discussions for social networking and support groups, but not video games. The neighborhood of the RER enjoyed the reputation of having clean air and of being a healthy place to live.

On the contrary, the control group had spent at least two hours watching TV every night before bedtime. They had slept only six hours at night, and they had spent a good amount of time during the day playing video games or riding on roller coasters and boats, instead of taking a nap. Each participant in the control group had also spent a minimum of six hours daily on the phone or around a computer. They would spend hours riding on motorcycles, cars, and buses in and around the NRER neighborhood. The neighborhood of the NRER hosted a large farm with tractors and other farming machines running on diesel around the clock. It also housed a chicken plant with heavy equipment. The NRER neighborhood was known for its pollution. The air quality in the NRER was poor or polluted, in part due to the emissions from the heavy equipment and the large number of buses, cars, and motorcycles traveling across the NRER neighborhood daily.

The results of the experiment showed that the type of energy source the participants depended on conditioned their lifestyle or habits to some degree, which ultimately affected their health. Their reliance on renewable energy source did not allow the participants in the treatment group long exposures to television; they washed their dishes manually, instead of using a dishwasher; their house had a small refrigerator to preserve food, and the renewable energy source made them run their heater low to save energy. They also enjoyed physical activities and cleaner air in the absence of motorcycles, cars, or heavy machinery.

Meanwhile, the participants in the control group could afford long hours watching television, due to perverse habits of lavish energy use encouraged by the non-renewable energy sources. They relied on a dishwasher for washing dishes, and they depended on a washer and dryer for laundry. Their house had a heating and cooling system running on high around the clock, and a huge refrigeration system served other related needs in the household. They also breathed a polluted air, in the midst of motorcycles, cars, and heavy machines.

Amazed by the differences or gaps between their experiences, Energia and her friends decided to spend another month in Choice City to replicate the experiment, by swapping the treatment group and the control group. The results were consistent for the next month, when Energia switched the two groups by assigning to the NRER neighborhood the subjects who spent the first month in the RER one and vice versa.

As per the first month of the experiment, at the end of the second month, the friends in the new study group (the RER group) reported a lower spending on electricity. The monthly amount spent on electricity for the new control group was three time higher than the one for the study group. Individual participants in the treatment group also reported lower stress level compared to those in the control group. At the end of the month, the systolic blood pressure, the pulse pressure, and the mean arterial blood pressure were significantly lower for the individuals in the RER neighborhood in comparison to those in the NRER control group. At the end of the second month, the recurrent experiment recorded a higher mean in the blood pressures of the individuals in the NRER control group, in comparison with the mean of the blood pressures of those in the RER treatment group.

In light of the results of the repeated experiment, as to how they confirmed that the type of energy source the experimentees relied on influenced their lifestyle and health, Energia would conclude mindfully in a significant statement:

"Maybe, the adoption of hydraulic energy could be a cornerstone to promoting or developing healthy sleeping habits. To some extent, energy source (or the type of energy we run on) contributes to the quality of some habits we develop with regard to lifestyle."

The results of the experiment reminded Energia of her ancestors' lifestyle in terms of how they had relied on the flowing waterbodies of rivers to produce clean energy for farming, and to grind grain in the olden days. She also remembered how her ancestors had developed good and healthy sleeping habits by following the cycle of the sun. They would go to bed with the sunset, and wake up with the sunrise. They felt healthy doing just that. Because they did not have sunlight at night, they did not work at night, they were not tempted to work at night, and they rested better. Their nights were more restful, for their nights were for sleeping and not for working.

The results of the experiment also inspired Energia to follow up with surveys for validation. At that turning point, her advisor would remind her tenaciously: "Be mindful that a survey is a quantitative method for acquiring knowledge through closed-ended questions or techniques in data collection and analysis."

With Chercheur's assistance, she designed a series of surveys to investigate the extent to which the citizens of Choice City would agree with increases in the city spending in the two areas of hydraulic energy and fossil fuel energy. She prepared a questionnaire that defined and coded the variables of her survey. The two main variables were *an increase in the city budget for hydraulic energy* and *an increase in the city budget for fossil fuel energy*. She would use a four-point scale to code the two variables respectively, with:

> One (1) meaning *to strongly disagree,*
> Two (2) meaning *to disagree,*
> Three (3) meaning *to agree,*
> Four (4) meaning *to strongly agree.*

On the questionnaire, she invited the participants to consider the two kinds of energy carefully and decide their level of agreement with a decision of the city to increase spending in either case. The participants would indicate their level of agreement in each case by circling a number on the four-point scale. Other variables on the questionnaire included the gender of the potential participants (as males or females), and the age of each participant in years. Energia coded the females as *1* and the males as *2*, meaning a female respondent would circle *1*, while a male respondent would circle *2*, to indicate their respective gender.

Chercheur would advise Energia to draft an informed consent form for conducting cross-sectional and longitudinal surveys.

Though she knew what a consent form was, Energia had no clue what Chercheur meant by cross-sectional and longitudinal surveys.

"What do you mean by cross-sectional and longitudinal surveys?" she asked keenly.

"A cross-sectional survey," he answered, "is the type where you survey the participants only once, without any follow-up. It has the benefit not to bother the participants with follow-up investigations. In contrast, a longitudinal survey calls for follow-ups. The follow-up investigations or checkups host the benefits of expanding the study to boost its reliability and validity."

He also explained that Energia could opt for multiple modes to conduct the surveys. One option could be to do the surveys by printing and mailing the questionnaire to the participants; another one could be to survey by calling the participants on the phone, asking them questions; she could choose to email the questions to the participants. She could also select to meet the participants one-on-one for in-person questioning.

Following a meticulous survey design that had taken into account Chercheur's advice, Energia printed more than a hundred copies of the questionnaire, and she carried them with copies of the consent form to a local and random shopping mall for an in-person investigation among a population of shoppers. Mindful of her mentor's recommendations, she set a table in a small corner of the large shopping mall and distributed copies of the questionnaire to the shoppers passing by, asking them to complete the survey freely, in case they had consented to participate. Scores of enthusiastic shoppers would accept to participate in the surveys by filling out the forms.

She spent the entire day surveying shoppers randomly. Many of them returned their completed questionnaires to her table. She was happy to collect those responses. She was also grateful to each respondent. In addition to granting a very warm smile to every respondent, along with a thank-you card, she would also reward each of them with a gift card to express her appreciation for the information, all in the end of showing reciprocity, consistent with the rules of ethical concerns in data collection and in research. She ensured the participants understood she valued the information they had provided so generously. By the end of the day, she would survey a sample of hundred adult shoppers. She had targeted adults only to avoid potential issues of ethical considerations involving the participation of minors.

The results of the surveys would show fifty female participants (which represented fifty percent of the sample) and fifty male participants (which corresponded to fifty percent of the sample). The participants were twenty-one years and older. The respondents had a mean age of thirty-four. For the two variables of *'increase in the city budget for hydraulic energy'* and *'increase in the city budget for fossil fuel energy,'* the results showed that support for an *increase in the city budget for hydraulic energy* was highest among the citizens of Choice City. Most of the citizens strongly supported an increased city spending on hydropower, mainly because of some tangible benefits of hydroelectricity.

Not too long after, Energia would follow up on the phone with respondents who had consented to participate in a longitudinal study, to further examine what had motivated their strong support for an increased budget for hydraulic energy in Choice City. The follow-up surveys showed several respondents who relied on the fossil fuel energy complained about expensive monthly electric bills, in comparison to their fellows who were dependent on hydroelectricity. The results of the longitudinal surveys would reflect the citizens' perceptions about the advantages of relying on hydroelectricity in Choice City, in terms of how hydroelectric barrages helped counter the risks of flooding in the city, how they contributed to water conservation or preservation for drinking and irrigation. The results also unveiled other benefits relating to low CO_2 emissions; hydropower generators did not seem to emit air pollutants in Choice City. The surveys also revealed that citizens' awareness of potential disadvantages of hydroelectric dams to the environment (for example, the destructive impact on fish and some other living beings) did not deter them from endorsing the usage of hydropower; they believed its benefits to be higher than its costs.

A week later, Energia would extend her investigations to another city nearby, with a different set of surveys. It was in Water City, a small city running solely on hydropower. The city was adjacent to the major river crossing Choice City. It was also the home of a small number of lakes and other streams. Beside its flowing waterbodies, its beautiful botanical and zoological gardens provided a paradise for walkers and visitors. Energia enjoyed her short sojourn in Water City; she felt the city was truly a small haven of happiness. The standards of living were decent in Water City, the cost of living was relatively cheap. Its citizens' inexpensive and relaxed lifestyle made the city the favorite destination for many retirees in the region. Water City hosted several popular retirement communities with a vested interest in the practice of yoga or other techniques of meditation.

The purpose of Energia's surveys was to examine the extent to which the residents of Water City were satisfied with their usage of hydroelectricity and how hydropower energy affected their lifestyle. To that end, she developed a survey questionnaire made of closed-ended questions and a four-point scale.

Her closed-ended questions included the following:

"Are you happy, living in Water City?"

"Do you think the source of energy you rely on contributes to your happiness?"

"Are you satisfied with depending on hydropower as your source of energy?"

"Do you prefer hydraulic energy as your source of electricity, when compared with the fossil fuel energy?"

"Do you think hydroelectricity is cheaper in comparison to the fossil fuel energy?

"Would you recommend hydroelectric power to some other cities?"

Upon Chercheur's advice, Energia would also insert an open-ended question to record additional and opportunistic data for a triangulation. She included the following question:

"How would you compare life in Water City to life in another city you had lived in previously?"

Shortly afterwards, she came back at her mentor with a subsequent question.

"What is a triangulation?" she asked him impetuously.

"In the context of research in the social sciences," he explained rhetorically, "a triangulation refers to a strategy for combining both quantitative and qualitative techniques concurrently in the process of data collection and analysis. It is a popular methodology you can use to mix or integrate systematically quantitative and qualitative data in any scientific investigation. It provides a comprehensive and balanced understanding of social reality, as it relies concomitantly on the strengths of qualitative and quantitative tools for reliability and validity."

In light of that explanation, Energia thought it was significant to adopt such a multimethod approach for substantial and valid outcomes.

"Triangulation seems to be a strategy of the utmost importance in this case!" she exclaimed enthusiastically. "It adds both depth and scope to my research; it boosts my own credulity and the credibility of the results to the fullest."

Once again, she was grateful to her advisor for his thoughtfulness.

On the survey questionnaire, she had defined the variable of happiness as a *disposition granting the peace of heart and mind*. As her rule of thumb, a subject's happiness depended on all the following criteria taken together:

You live in an environment where the air is not polluted.

You sleep at least eight hours at night.

You have at least one hour to take a nap after lunch daily.

You do not experience headaches daily.

You have at least an hour to walk in the nature, in the countryside, daily.

You eat colorful food daily.

You have access to clean water and drink healthy water daily.

You are not overwhelmed by monthly bills.

The survey design would use a four-point scale to code the variable 'satisfaction with hydroelectricity':

One (1) meaning *very dissatisfied with hydroelectricity,*
Two (2) meaning *dissatisfied with hydroelectricity,*
Three (3) meaning *satisfied with hydroelectricity,*
Four (4) meaning *very satisfied with hydroelectricity.*

On the questionnaire, Energia encouraged the participants to express their level of satisfaction with the usage of hydroelectricity. The participants would indicate their level of satisfaction by circling a number on the four-point scale.

Other variables on the questionnaire included the gender of the potential respondents (as males or females), and the age of each respondent in years. She coded the females as 1 and the male as 2, meaning a female respondent would circle 1, and a male would circle 2, to reflect their respective gender.

After a careful survey design, she printed more than a hundred copies of the questionnaire, and she carried them with copies of the consent form to a local and random recreational park in Water City for an in-person investigation among a population of retirees. She set up a tent in a small corner of the park and handed out copies of the questionnaire to the residents walking by, asking them to freely complete the survey, after they had consented to participate.

Many walkers accepted to fill out the forms and participate in the surveys eagerly. Energia would spend the entire day surveying the strollers randomly. A large number of respondents would return their completed questionnaires to the tent. She expressed her gratitude to them, by rewarding each respondent with a written thank-you card and a gift card for appreciation and reciprocity. By the end of the day, Energia would survey a sample of one hundred retirees. She targeted residents who had moved from a different city to Water City to allow the data to reflect a comparison between their previous city of residence and Water City.

Per the results of the surveys, there were fifty female respondents (which represented fifty percent of the sample) and fifty male respondents (which represented fifty percent of the sample). The respondents were sixty-five years and older; they had a mean age of sixty-eight. Ninety percent of the respondents were very satisfied with relying on hydroelectric power in Water City. Ten percent indicated they were satisfied with using hydroelectricity. The one hundred respondents reported they were happy living in Water City. All the respondents indicated that the source of energy they depended on contributed to their happiness. They all expressed satisfaction with relying on hydropower as their source of energy. They all preferred hydraulic energy as their source of electricity compared to hydrocarbon fuels. They reported hydroelectricity was cheaper in comparison with the fossil fuels energy. They indicated they would recommend hydroelectric power to other cities. The results translated meaningfully some impacts of the usage of hydroelectric power on a happy lifestyle. Relying on hydropower certainly hosts some potentials for happiness.

The open-ended question had allowed a few respondents to provide some relative narratives. One respondent's perspective was particularly catchy. An Eighty-one-year-old respondent by the name of Yonhonon indicated she had spent some years of her life next to a popular lake in the kingdom of Energium, prior to moving to Water City. The lake was called Nonto. Yonhonon's narrative would reveal detrimental impacts of the digital currency on the natural environments.

"I was born and raised on the bay of the lake!" she said. "Growing up next to Lake Nonto was a beautiful and healthy experience. When I was a teenager, my parents used to take us to Nonto for swimming. Its freshwater was clear and clean. During the summer, hundreds of people would congregate to Nonto every day to contemplate its beautiful sceneries and refresh their minds. Residents living nearby would fetch drinking water from the lake. Nonto was home to a wide variety of water creatures, including fish, shrimp, crabs, oysters, turtles, and other aquatic creatures. My father was fond of fishing its white bass, trout, and catfish for delightful lunches in the weekends. My mother enjoyed catching its shrimp and oyster for delicious dinners. The trees standing by Nonto were all green, and the overall adjacent vegetation was luxuriant. The bayside environment was friendly and healthy; it was the habitat for squirrels, lizards, chameleons, iguanas, snakes, dragonflies, and more living creatures. I had witnessed ducks, geese, parrots, owls, pigeons, sparrows, eagles, and other types of birds rush to Lake Nonto to quench their thirst. Dozens of butterflies played happily on the flowers in the vicinity of the lake. Near Nonto, you would breathe clean air. It was a place of happiness."

"Unfortunately," she went on, "all that would change suddenly in my seventies, after a major corporation had built a cryptocurrency mining plant on the shoreline of the lake. Over the following years, the environmental conditions in and around Nonto grew increasingly fraught with xeric or xerothermic hardship. It only took a few years for Nonto and its bay to shift from a friendly and healthy environment to a hostile and unhealthy one. A couple of years following the installation of the plant, the waters of Nonto started heating up. We could no longer swim in the lake or drink its water. Residents who dared take a sip of the water got sick or died. The wildlife perished dramatically inside the waters and by the lakeside. Thousands of water creatures died, including plants, fish, and other living beings inside the waters. Hundreds of birds died by the waterside. The leaves of the trees on the bank became yellow or orange. The evergreen trees on the shore traded their foliage for a brown discoloration: some turned brown, others dried up. The bayside vegetation slowly vanished. I witnessed the destructive change with sadness. The environmental obliteration was patent and heartbreaking. It was a catastrophe for the flora and fauna of Lake Nonto; it was bad news for ecology and biodiversity."

"As a worried and very concerned resident," she continued, "I decided to research the potential factors which could have contributed to that drastic and dramatic alteration. As I investigated the issue, I figured out that the one and only different thing that had occurred around Nonto over those years of my life was the intrusion of the cryptocurrency firm; I discovered that the only new catalyzing factor or major intervening variable in that environment was the digital currency plant. I set to scrutinize the relationship between cryptocurrency plant and environmental pollution. What I found was petrifying. As I collected and examined data, my data analysis showed a positive and statistically significant correlation between the two variables of cryptocurrency mining plant and environmental pollution. Per my own life experiences and observations in the environment of Lake Nonto, there was a severe increase in air pollution and water pollution with the advent of the cryptocurrency mining farm. The emission levels of greenhouse gases such as carbon dioxide and chlorofluorocarbons skyrocketed, with harmful impacts on the climate."

"Some of my findings were quite shocking," she persisted. "It turned out that cryptocurrency transactions required extremely high demands in energy. The cryptocurrency plant on the bank of Lake Nonto used about twenty-five megawatts of power, primarily from burning the fossil fuels, mainly the coal. The cooling system of that digital currency plant would pump and use the freshwater from Nonto and release it back at a temperature of ninety-five degrees Fahrenheit. Obviously, this temperature would kill plenty of white bass, trout, and other water creatures, while it fostered the development of harmful algae blooms in Nonto. Many residents would get sick with cancer, including myself. From experiencing a chronic xerosis, I ended up with a sink cancer and a lung cancer. It did not take me long to understand that I had to run away for my life. Fortunately, I have found refuge in Water City, a healthier environment, a paradise of clean water and air."

"Regrettably," he admitted, "the fact that many young citizens in the demographic cohort of the zoomers or Generation Z believe in cryptocurrency seems to add insult to injury. Our zoomers represent the global leaders of tomorrow, and their inclination to or faith in digital currency darkens the horizon and dims our hopes in the future."

"The earth hangs in tatters in many regions, due to the immoderate human consumption of the fossil fuels," she concluded somberly. "Our excessive usage of the hydrocarbon fuels is a recipe for disaster, a hazardous choice fraught with all the ingredients of a planetary destruction. Our addiction to non-renewable energy makes us engage in a perilous zero-sum game in which we win energy for the short term to the detriment of our health in the long term. But, let us face it: is this venture really worth it? No, it is not, it is rather worthless. It makes no sense to trade environmental and public health for short-lived wins in hydrocarbon energy; in the end we gain nothing, but we lose everything. Yet we still have some chances and the means to reverse the current trend."

Yonhonon's reflective narrative visibly touched Energia, it warned her of the negative effects of digital currency on the natural environment.

Overall, Energia thought the results of data collection and analysis in Water City were impressive and fulfilling. She enjoyed not only those results but also the quality of her time in Water City. The pace of life was very relaxed, and she got to spend some good time with the senior citizens. She would take advantage of the slow pace and seize the opportunity of her time with the elderly for further data collection.

Toward the end of her stay in Water City, she designed another survey to obtain additional data. Through brainstorming, she identified and wrote down up to fifty popular opinions on (or potential explanations of) global warming and climate change on the minds of the youth and senior citizens. Her ultimate goal was to test those opinions scientifically for reliable and valid explanations of global warming and climate change. The long list of opinions included, but was not limited to, the following ones:

"I think gas emissions from cars contribute to global warming and climate change,"

"It seems to me that emissions from airplanes lead to global warming and climate change,"

"I blame industrial emissions for global warming and climate change,"

"I think plastic disposals are conducive to global warming and climate change,"

"I suspect poor garbage disposals contribute to global warming and climate change,"

"I can tell wildfires lead to global warming and climate change,"

"I think cremating dead bodies contributes to global warming and climate change,"

"I blame the use of pesticides partly for global warming and climate change,"

"I predict gases and substances such as mercury and arsenic contribute to climate change,"

"I imagine that agriculture or farming contributes to global warming and climate change,"

"I have no doubt that chemical wastes lead to global warming and climate change,"

"I believe hospital wastes could foster global warming and climate change,"

"I understand chemical leaks or spills contribute to global warming and climate change,"

"I think fracking and oil cracking lead to global warming and climate change,"

"I believe pharmaceutical wastes contribute to global warming and climate change,"

"I predict all forms of oil and gas production lead to global warming and climate change,"

"I think gas stations and distribution processes foster global warming and climate change,"

"I imagine burning gasoline increases the chances of global warming and climate change,"

"It seems to me that oil spills can contribute to global warming and climate change,"

"I blame the coal plants for global warming and climate change,"

"I suspect nuclear plants foster global warming and climate change,"

"I have no doubt wars and heavy weaponry lead to global warming and climate change,"

"I think atomic explosions maximize the probability of global warming and climate change,"

"I suspect deforestation contributes to global warming and climate change,"

"I blame radioactive materials for global warming and climate change,"

"I think there are many human activities leading to global warming and climate change,"

"I imagine non-human activities contribute to global warming and climate change."

Energia would use a four-point scale to rate each of the fifty opinions, with:

1 meaning to *strongly disagree* with the opinion,

2 meaning to *disagree* with the opinion,

3 meaning to *agree* with the opinion,

4 meaning to *strongly agree* with the opinion.

Out of the random sample of one hundred retirees who had volunteered to participate in that survey, ninety-six respondents turned in their answers. Satisfied with the great turnout, Energia happily welcomed the completed surveys with gratitude. She would store them safely before leaving Water City for the kingdom of Energium.

On her way back to Energium, as she leafed through the data, aflame with passion for her research, and in anticipation of the data analysis and results, she thought to herself, *"If you do not know or have not experienced any other alternatives in existence, you tend to think that your current option is unique or the best. But there are multiple interesting options actually, and none of them is the best. Yet some other options are well worth trying, for learning, change, or growth."*

A few weeks later, upon Chercheur's request and under his guidance, she would use a method called *factor analysis* to run the data.

CHAPTER 5

Energia's Data Analysis Methods and Results

Upon their return to Energium, Chercheur would advise Energia to perform a content analysis on the newspapers of the kingdom to make sense of the main debate topics across the nation. This would help both him and her update themselves, after a long absence from Energium.

"What is a content analysis?" she asked him.

"You conduct a content analysis," he said, "whenever you study the content of any recorded communication. It could be the content of a photo album, a stamp album, a sticker album, an autograph album, a musical album, a song, a painting, a book, a journal, a magazine, a newspaper, a website, a letter, a text message, or an email."

"How do I perform the content analysis of newspapers in the case of my research?" she asked, both responsively and adumbratively.

"Listen, and make a mental note of it!" he exclaimed oratorically. "First, you come up with a research hypothesis, a general opinion or statement you would like to test. Once you have a hypothesis, you need to identify the dependent variable in the hypothesis and create at least two categories to operationalize or measure the dependent variable. Coding your categories numerically will help the analysis tremendously. After you have identified the groups in your dependent variable, you need to identify the unit of analysis, which is the small subset you focus on for data collection. In this case, your unit of analysis is article, I mean the articles in the newspapers. Next, you choose a time period, and you randomly select a newspaper to start reading its articles. For example, if your hypothesis is that *the articles from newspapers in Energium echo the debate on renewable energy*, as you read each article, you identify whether it is about renewable energy or not. If, for instance, you get more than fifty percent of the articles reflecting the topic of renewable energy, then you will conclude that renewable energy represents the main topic being debated in the kingdom, which would support your research hypothesis and reject the null hypothesis."

To heed her mentor's advice, Energia set to discover the trends in social debates in the Kingdom of Energium through a content analysis. She would randomly select a sample of one hundred local newspapers and monitor them to uncover local trends of publications. She started the process of the content analysis by conceptualizing two broad categories to classify the topics covered in the newspapers. Her first category was on the *newspapers with at least one article on the benefits of renewable energy sources*. She coded that group numerically as one (1). The second category was on the *newspapers without any allusion to renewable energy*, which she coded as zero (0). As she leafed through the newspapers, she found that seventy-five out of the one hundred newspapers had at least one article on the benefits of promoting renewable energies.

Encouraged by those findings, she decided to take a step further in the content analysis. She randomly selected ten of the one hundred newspapers and read all their articles. She wanted to test the hypothesis that the articles in the newspapers reflected the need to promote renewable energies. At this stage, she would create three thematic rubrics to organize the articles in the newspapers she had selected. The first rubric was on *articles without any allusion to energy sources*, the second was on *articles advocating for non-renewable energy sources*, and the third one was on *articles in favor of renewable energy sources*. She coded the three rubrics, using a numerical logic. The rubric on *articles without any allusion to energy sources* received the number 0 as its code. The rubric on *articles advocating for non-renewable energy sources* got the number 1 as its code. She assigned the number 2 as a code to the rubric on *articles in favor of renewable energy sources*.

Out of the two hundred ninety-eight articles contained in the ten newspapers, one hundred fifty-four articles examined the benefits of renewable energies and advocated for the need to promote renewable energy sources. Ninety-three other articles did not allude in any way to energy sources. Only fifty-one of the two hundred ninety-eight articles backed some advantages of non-renewable energy sources. The results showed that the category coded as 2 was the most dominant, meaning that the articles supporting renewable energy sources had the highest coverage in the newspapers, which confirmed Energia's research hypothesis.

In light of those results, she got a clear message: she was not alone in the kingdom of Energium to think about the urgent need to promote renewable energy sources. She understood that the data collected from the newspapers echoed the voices of many citizens of the kingdom. She assumed that such relevant data reflected her fellow citizens' concerns and wishes clearly. She felt comforted to understand that many of the citizens of Energium were supportive of renewable energies. The results of the content analysis would reassure Energia that she was fighting for a good cause. She felt happy that she was on the right path with her research initiative.

In view of the results of the content analysis, she drew near Chercheur and whispered in his ears, "Content analysis is very helpful for data processing. I really appreciate your guidance through this useful method."

As she expressed her gratitude to him for advising her on performing a content analysis, Chercheur said, "Indeed, content analysis is a convenient method to process and analyze any recorded data, including data from diaries or journals, minutes of meetings, book reports or reviews, observations, interviews, and surveys. In the specific case of your research, you could use it to analyze the data you had collected from your observations, interviews, and surveys for meaning making. You could also do a content analysis of your personal diaries to apprehend or comprehend your recorded experiences about renewable and non-renewable energies."

Chercheur was mindful to alert Energia on the strengths and weaknesses of content analysis. He said, "Content analysis would save you time and money; it is a relatively cheap, quick, and easy research method. You can conduct it behind your computer in record time. However, it only applies to recorded oral, written, or painted communications; you cannot use it for non-recorded communications. It tends to be superficial, as it proceeds by quantitative word counts generally. It does not perform an in-depth analysis that digs into the innuendos, the feelings behind the words used, and their meanings."

"Which other methods would you advise for data analysis?" she asked him.

"I have a plethora of them boggling my mind right now," he joked.

She motioned to him to spell them out: "Why don't you spit them out, sir?" she jested.

"Certainly!" he answered. "I would encourage narrative analysis, comparative analysis (including t-test for independent groups, paired-sample t-test, and analysis of variance), correlation analysis, regression analysis, and factor analysis. The list could be longer, but you can focus on those ones."

"What could you tell me about narrative analysis?" she asked.

"Narrative analysis is the study of a narration," he replied. "It scrutinizes written and verbal communications."

"I find it hard to differentiate between content analysis and narrative," she complained.

"Content analysis and narrative analysis," he said, "are similar to some degree, they both analyze human communications, by examining who said what to whom, how, and why. The difference between the two resides mainly in the depth of narrative analysis. While content analysis often remains on the surface of the words by focusing more on counting the manifest words to make conclusions based on the frequency of their usage or the number of times they appear in the narration, narrative analysis descends deeply inside the words to understand and exhibit their meanings and effects."

"Please explain further what you mean," she interjected.

"Narrative analysis," he went on, "is highly interpretative; it emphasizes more meticulously the underlying assumptions and meanings of the words, by capturing the details of a written communication, including the meanings of punctuations and insinuations. In a spoken communication, narrative analysis reflects on the pauses, the eye contact, the facial expression, the gestures, the emotions, and other non-verbal attitudes occurring in the communication."

"How would you illustrate the use of narrative analysis in the case of my study?" she interrupted.

"You could well apply narrative analysis to your diaries or journals," he said. "You can use it to analyze the daily records of events and experiences you have been keeping. You can also perform a narrative analysis of the transcripts of your interviews on the benefits of wind energy in Wind City, by reflecting on the specifics of the narratives of the respondents, including the meanings of their words, their voice tones, their emotions, their gestures, and their hems and haws."

Motivated by Chercheur's suggestions, Energia would read through the transcripts of the interviews she had conducted in Wind City to organize the narratives and code them thematically. She would also listen to the narratives she had recorded in Wind City to understand the meanings of the respondents' facial expressions, their gestures, their emotions, their pauses, or the hems and haws. She would engage in a double process of conceptualization and operationalization of the interviews.

After spending much of her time reading and listening to the transcripts of the interviews, she conceptualized and created two coding categories to classify the data from the interviews. The first coded category was about the health benefits of wind energy in Wind City. The second coded category was on the economic benefits of wind energy in Wind City. As she analyzed the narratives from the interviews, she identified clear indicators for each coded category. The indicators of health benefits included low CO_2 emissions, breathing clean air, feeling relaxed, feeling healthier physically and mentally, and feeling happy. The indicators of economic benefits included the affordability of wind energy with citizens spending less money on electric bills, and the high employment rates in the sector of wind energy. The two sets of qualitative indicators mirrored the respondents' multidimensional experience in terms of the benefits they had harnessed from wind energy.

Energia's tight scrutiny of the interviewees' facial expressions, tones, gestures, emotions, and pauses was amenable to clarifying the underlying assumptions of the narratives. The coding operations contributed to a better understanding of the latent or hidden content of the interviews in reference to the social and economic benefits of wind energy for the citizens of Wind City.

Satisfied with the results of her conceptualization and operationalization of the interviews, she exclaimed, "Wow! What a helpful method narrative analysis is!"

Chercheur nodded his head in agreement. "It is very useful for meaning making!" he exclaimed.

"What about comparative analysis?" she asked him.

"I would present comparative analysis," he said, "as a process that allows a researcher to examine and compare two or more social units, objects, individuals, groups, cases, events, processes, interventions, documents, variables, or data sets. Though it can be qualitative as in situations of small-number cases (less than ten cases), it is often quantitative, because it covers a large number of cases (ten or more cases)."

"Could you specify and explain some quantitative tests for comparative analysis?" she interposed.

"Absolutely," he said. "We could think of the independent t-test, the paired-samples t-test, and the one-way analysis of variance, to name a few tests used for comparison."

"How would you define the independent t-test?" she asked. "When and how can I use it?"

"The independent t-test," he said, "allows you to compare two independent groups, by testing the differences between the means of the two groups. For example, you could use the independent t-test to examine the effects of non-renewable energy in comparison to the effects of renewable energy on the environment. You could also rely on the independent t-test to compare if the men and women of the kingdom of Energium differ in their interest in renewable energy. Be mindful the independent t-test applies to cases where you compare only two independent groups. If you have more than two independent groups, you cannot use that test."

"That is interesting!" she exclaimed. "What about the paired-samples t-test?"

"The paired-samples t-test," he said, "allows you to compare pairs, or matching objects or subjects. Whereas the independent t-test requires independent groups, the paired-samples t-test requires matched groups or correlated groups. In practice, the paired-samples t-test involves a pre-test and a post-test design. For instance, you could use the paired-samples t-test to analyze the data from the experiment you had conducted in Choice City on the benefits of renewable energy."

"This conversation is so helpful," she interrupted. "How about the one-way analysis of variance?"

"The one-way analysis of variance," he replied, "allows the researcher to compare three or more independent groups. Remember what I said previously about the independent t-test. If you are interested in comparing more than two groups, you cannot use the independent t-test to achieve your goal; the one-way analysis of variance is the tool for this level of comparison. For example, you can use the one-way analysis of variance to find out whether the type of energy source an automobile relies on would affect the level of air pollution in the environment."

"This is all exciting," she interjected."

Excited and inspired by Chercheur's explanations, Energia decided to spend the rest of that day applying the independent t-test, the paired-samples t-test, and the one-way analysis of variance to analyze the data she had collected in Sun City, Wind City, Choice City, and Water City.

She resolved to compare the monthly direct and well-to-wheel carbon emissions of gasoline-powered vehicles to the monthly carbon emissions of electric vehicles. She defined direct vehicle carbon emission as the carbon a vehicle would produce through its tailpipe and the carbon evaporating through fueling. She defined well-to-wheel emissions as the carbon from the vehicle using energy, as well as the carbon from the production, processing, and distribution of the vehicle and the energy it would use (whether it is electric energy or gasoline). In her perspective, the well-to-wheel emissions do not include the recycling process or disposal of the vehicle. Energia would include the disposal or recycling in another broader variable, one of the life cycle emissions of the vehicle. She perceived the life cycle emissions of a vehicle as encompassing the overall emissions relating to the production, the distribution, the operation, and the disposal or recycling of the vehicle and the energy it would use. She did not consider the variable of life cycle emissions in this analysis.

For the purposes of her study, Energia would use the independent t-test to analyze the data from a major automobile company in Choice City. The data set she relied on presented the city's monthly averages of carbon emissions per vehicle and measured the carbon dioxide emissions in metric pounds for a sample of one thousand vehicles, including five hundred electric vehicles and five hundred gasoline-operating vehicles. The comparison revealed significant differences between the mean of the electric vehicles and the vehicles running on gasoline.

The results indicated that the electric vehicles had no direct carbon emission during operation. The gasoline-powered vehicles had high direct carbon emissions through their tailpipes and through evaporating fuel. The results also showed that electric vehicles had lower well-to-wheel carbon emissions compared to gasoline-powered vehicles. The relatively low carbon emissions associated with electric vehicles came not from their tailpipes, but from the electric power plants and the process of production and distribution of the electricity they used.

Energia would also use the independent t-test for testing how the male and female citizens of Sun City would agree with an increase in the city budget for solar energy. She randomly selected a sample of one hundred citizens of Sun City, including fifty males and fifty females. She would ask them to express their level of agreement with the increase on a scale of one (*1*) to four (*4*), with:

1 meaning strongly disagree,
2 meaning disagree,
3 meaning agree,
4 meaning strongly agree.

The results of the analysis showed a major difference between the females and males. The mean for the female citizens was greater than the mean for the male citizens. The support for increased spending for solar energy was higher among the female than the male citizens of Sun City.

She decided subsequently to examine whether first-time male and female drivers in Energium would differ in their inclination to driving electric cars or gasoline-powered cars. She randomly selected fifty first-time female drivers and fifty first-time male drivers from a population of

Generation Z drivers in Energium. She would ask all one hundred drivers to choose between driving an electric vehicle and a vehicle running on gasoline. She would use the independent t-test to compare the means of the two groups. The analysis revealed a significant difference between the females and males. The mean for the female drivers was greater than the mean for the male drivers. Per the mean values, significantly more female drivers preferred driving electric cars than male drivers.

Obviously satisfied with the results of her t-tests analyses, Energia would extend her analytical efforts, by applying the technics of the one-way analysis of variance (ANOVA) to find out the differences in the levels of air pollution by electric vehicles, hybrid vehicles, and vehicles operating solely on gasoline. In that perspective, she would rely on the same data she had previously used, from the automobile company in Choice City. She defined the level of air pollution as the amount of greenhouse gases and other air pollutants (measured in metric tons) vehicles released in the natural environment annually. She would rank the levels of air pollution as low (coded as 1), medium (coded as 2), and high (coded as 3). The electric vehicles relied on electric power one hundred percent. The hybrid vehicles had both an electric mode and a combustible mode. The gasoline-powered vehicles ran exclusively on gasoline.

She performed the analysis over one hundred and fifty vehicles, including fifty electric vehicles, fifty hybrid vehicles, and fifty gasoline-powered vehicles. The mean values for the three groups of vehicles indicated that the vehicles running on gasoline had the highest emissions of carbon dioxide, methane, nitrous oxide, and other air pollutants such as nitrogen oxides. The hybrid vehicles followed with a medium level of emissions of carbon dioxide, methane, and nitrogen oxides. The electric vehicles came last with the lowest levels. The results of the analysis showed that the type of energy source a vehicle used had a significant impact on the level of air pollution, meaning that the vehicles running solely on gasoline polluted the air more than the hybrid vehicles, and far more than the electric vehicles. The analysis enhanced that the electric vehicles running on electricity from wind or solar energy recorded lower well-to-wheel or life cycle emissions, when compared to the electric vehicles running on electricity from coal and natural gas. On a side note, the analysis signaled that electric vehicles were quieter than vehicles operating on petrol or diesel, which provides a good remedy for noise pollution. In light of those results, she concluded that the electric vehicles were good for a clean environment and public health.

At the end of that day, Energia happily presented the results of the different analyses to her advisor for his feedback.

It was late, and Chercheur advised her to go rest.

She gave a deep groan, left reluctantly, and went back home.

The same was not true of her advisor. He withdrew to his office quietly, and spent some time reviewing the results of Energia's data analysis. As he read through the analysis, feasting his eyes of the findings, his phone rang.

It was his wife, Luz.

"The children and I are waiting, I hope you are joining us for dinner today?" she said desperately.

Apparently surprised, Chercheur looked up. It was eight o'clock; he was due back home at six o'clock for dinner with his family.

"I am very sorry, Sweetheart!" he said to his wife. "It is my mistake, I am leaving my office right now."

"You mean you are still in your office at this time," interrupted Luz, "I hope everything is fine."

"I got hooked on reviewing the results of Energia's data analyses, and the time had slipped by quickly, it is my mistake," he replied remorsefully.

"It happens; setting your alarm as a reminder could help you regulate your passion for research, for a balanced lifestyle."

Chercheur got the message, and on his way out, he set his alarm right away for the following day.

Back to his house, he rushed through the entrance, and before Luz and their two children could welcome him back in, he said to them in a soft voice, "My dear wife, son, and daughter, I know I owe you all a thousand apologies. I am very sorry."

His daughter Mira replied teasingly, "Let this be a warning for you, Mr. Researcher! Be punctual in the future, or you will get a fine, a probation, or a sentence."

Her joke made their entire family giggle.

"No," Chercheur interrupted with an emotional plea, "I may be able to handle a fine with your mother's assistance, but I do not want a sentence, and I cannot afford a probation away from my lovely and loving family."

"Be reassured I have learned from my mistake, and I promise sincerely to make up for this," he added apologetically.

In the blink of an eye, Luz gave her husband an affectionate hug and covered his face with kisses. Mira and her brother Stellus followed suit, and the family moved to the dining room to enjoy a late dinner peacefully.

Chercheur was very grateful to Luz for her understanding and helpful tip.

Early in the morning, the next day, apparently satisfied with the results of the data analyses, he gave Energia high marks, but he added,

"Though your analysis reveals that the electric vehicles release less nitrogen oxides and less greenhouse gases such as carbon monoxide and methane, it also sounds the alarm on the roots or sources of electricity. Depending on their electricity sources, electric vehicles more than gasoline vehicles could have a greater acidification effect on the environment; their production processes and the manufacture of their batteries demand greater quantities of toxic minerals, including copper, nickel, and aluminum. This red flag reminds you that electric vehicles do not represent a perfect recipe for environmental health. So, don't be fooled, be on your guard against any glamorous lure!

"Your analysis also seemed to shed light on another significant difference. Driving electric vehicles in geographic locations of Choice City that relied heavily on non-renewable energy sources, such as the fossil fuels, to generate electricity did not result in easily detectable and quantifiable direct emissions of greenhouse gases. Meanwhile, when driven in the neighborhood running on renewable energy, the electric vehicles clearly recorded zero direct carbon emission."

He quickly followed up with positive comments when he said to Energia, "You show proficiency not only in data collection but also in data analysis. This illustrates how you develop your research skills by applying the research strategies you learn. Well done! You make considerable progress, and you earn full credit for it. I know you can do better by going even further."

"I appreciate your compliments," she replied tactfully, "I can go further only with your help."

"At your service!" he exclaimed. "I am glad I can help."

"How may I assist you?" he asked subsequently.

She giggled and said jokingly, "I will appreciate it, if your Highness can now lead me through the other analytical tools you had mentioned previously."

"Could you be more specific?" he requested.

"I need your help to understand correlation analysis, regression analysis, time-series analysis, and factor analysis," Energia responded.

Chercheur said, "Well! I understand correlation analysis as a test for a possible relationship between two variables at a minimum, by examining the magnitude of that relationship and its direction as positive or negative. You could perform a correlation analysis to determine the extent and direction of the relationship between the two variables of energy source and air quality."

"How can I do that in practice?" she enquired, perplexed.

He looked at her to reassure her and said, "Using a computer program designed for data analysis, you can analyze statistically a pair of data on the two variables of *energy source* and *air quality* to find out if there is any relationship between the two and to determine the magnitude and direction of that relationship."

"What would indicate that the variables in the analysis correlate?" she wondered nervously.

He smiled to appease her and said, "Do not worry! By convention, we call it a *correlation coefficient*, the number that expresses the relationship between your variables. The correlation analysis will display the correlation coefficient as a number. That number may vary from -1 to +1."

"How do I interpret the negative one (*-1*) and the positive one (*+1*)?" she persisted.

He looked at her again and replied assuredly, "You will interpret -1 or +1 as a perfect relationship between the two variables (with respect to the magnitude of that relationship). The closer the correlation coefficient is to 1, the more significant the relationship between the variables. As a conventional rule or principle, the level of significance is usually set at less or equal to 0.05 in social research."

"What if the correlation coefficient stands at 0?" she continued insistently.

"That is a great question," he replied intently. "When the correlation coefficient is 0, this stance indicates the absence of a relationship between the variables."

Energia nodded and said, "How about the direction of that relationship? How do I determine if a relationship is positive or negative?"

Chercheur said, "The positive relationship means that the variables under study go in the same direction (the variables go together either east, or west, or south, or north, or up, or down, or high, or low). The correlation coefficient here shows a positive sign (as in + *0.513* or *0.513*). An example could be the positive relationship between *high blood pressure* and *high risk of heart attack*, or the positive correlation between *increase in stress* and *high cortisol levels*.

"The negative relationship implies that the variables go in different or opposite directions (when a variable moves east, the other one heads west; when one heads north, another one goes south; when one goes up or high, the other one heads down or low. The correlation coefficient shows a negative sign (as in - *0.479*). An example here could be the negative correlation between *high cholesterol* and *low-quality health*, or *high liver enzymes* and *decline in life expectancy*. In each case there is a relationship between the respective variables, but that relationship is negative.

"In the case of your study, if the *energy source* records high scores, while the *air quality* records high scores, this translates a positive relationship. When both the *energy source* and the *air quality* register low scores consistently, this also means a positive relationship between the two variables.

"However, when the *energy source* scores high, while the *air quality* scores low, this implies a negative relationship between the two variables. If the low scores of the *energy source* contrast the high scores of *the air quality*, this also means there is a negative relationship between the two variables."

"In the social sciences, we use different types of correlation coefficients," he went on, without breaking his train of thought. "The commonly used correlation coefficients include the *Pearson correlation coefficient* and the *Spearman correlation coefficient*. We use the *Pearson correlation coefficient* for scale (that is interval or ratio) variables such as age, income, weight, height, temperature, and other variables of the same kind. The *Spearman correlation coefficient* is for ordinal or ranking variables such as social class (as lower, middle, or upper class), rank of basketball team (as fourth, third, second, or first team), size of T-shirt (as small, medium, large, or extra-large size), the intensity of heat or pain (as low, medium, or high), and other similar variables. We use the lowercase *r* to symbolize the *Pearson correlation coefficient*, and the symbol *rho* to represent the *Spearman correlation coefficient.*"

Staring at Chercheur all this time, Energia exclaimed, "How about some illustrations!"

"Good for you," he answered. "Let's suppose there is a correlation between the two variables of *vehicle mileage* and *rate of greenhouse gas emissions*. If the strength of the correlation shows up as 0.645, it means the value of *r* is 0.645. Notice we use the lowercase *r* to indicate the correlation coefficient, because we are in the presence of two scale variables. Meanwhile, if there is a correlation between the two variables of *size of solar panel* and *level of electricity production*, we will express the correlation coefficient with the symbol *rho*, because the two variables in question are ranking. If the strength of the correlation is 0.723, it means the value of *rho* is 0.723. In both cases here, *r* and *rho* indicate positive statistically significant correlations."

After listening carefully to his magisterial or masterful explanation, Energia uttered her gratitude to Chercheur. "Thanks to you," she said. "I now understand correlation analysis as a valuable test for social research."

"What about regression analysis?" she continued enthusiastically.

Following a deep breath, he said convincingly, "Regression analysis is another test of the relationship between two or more variables. Unlike correlation analysis which focuses on the magnitude and direction of the relationship, regression analysis uses the relationship for prediction. For instance, if you know the scores of the energy source, regression analysis allows you to predict the scores of the air quality.

"Keep in mind there are various forms of regression analyses. Most commonly, you will hear about linear regression and multiple regression. A linear regression implies the possibility of representing the relationship between the two variables by a straight line; you could do this by using graphical techniques or statistical plots. A multiple regression allows you to predict a variable simply from knowing a series of other correlating variables. For example, you could use multiple regression to analyze how the variable of environmental health depends on many other predicting variables."

With her eyes fixed on her advisor, Energia said, "It seems to me that regression analysis implies correlation analysis to some degree; prediction presupposes there is a relationship between the variables. I hope my perspective is accurate."

"I understand your point," Chercheur responded. "Correlation analysis is a prerequisite to regression analysis. Regression analysis inherently encompasses correlation analysis somehow."

"How about time-series analysis?" she asked.

"I perceive time-series analysis," he answered, "as a test for changes in a variable over time. You could use time-series analysis to examine the changes in energy source over time in the human history and test the explanations or justifications for the trends. You can do this by relying on the data you had recorded in your personal journals. In practice, regression analysis is helpful in time-series analysis."

"That is very interesting," she said. "What about factor analysis?"

"Factor analysis," he replied, "is a test that reduces a large number of highly correlated predicting variables to a small number of independently representative groups or factors in order to explain the outcome variable."

After uttering a deep groan, she said, "That is difficult for me to understand, please illustrate!"

"Of course, I will," he responded. "Imagine that a large number of variables contribute to air pollution. Let's suppose those variables include emissions from cars, emissions from airplanes, industrial emissions, plastic disposals, poor managements of garbage, wildfires, pesticides, farming, chemical wastes from pharmaceutical laboratories and hospitals, chemical leaks or spills, fracking or hydraulic fracturing and oil extraction and production processes, gas stations, burning gasoline, oil spills, coal plants, nuclear plants, wars, atomic explosions, and many other variables. Suppose we have as many as fifty variables contributing to air pollution. That is a large number of variables. When you look at these variables closely you realize that some of them are redundant, or they correlate highly. For example, the three variables of *emissions from cars, emissions from airplanes,* and *burning gasoline* are redundant, because they boil down to greenhouse gas emissions. *Greenhouse gases* become the common denominator, a factor hosting multiple redundant variables. Factor analysis is a method that allows you to group such redundant variables under the umbrellas of common denominators or factors. So, in the case of your research, instead of having up to fifty variables, we could reduce them to only five factors, with each respective factor regrouping ten redundant variables."

"How do I know the weight of each respective variable in a factor?" she questioned.

"The computer output of a factor analysis generates numbers or coefficients that express how each variable relates to its factor; we call them the *factor loadings*," he answered promptly. "Also be mindful of what we call the *eigenvalue* or the ratio between the general shared change and the unique change an extracted factor provides. Ideally, in factor analysis the extracted factors displaying eigenvalues of 1 or higher are significant, the analysis would disregard factors displaying eigenvalues less than 1. When the eigenvalue is higher than 1, it means that the extracted factor explains more of the general common change than the unique or specific change."

"I anticipate you may struggle to understand what I mean by *eigenvalues*, but do not worry, you will understand it better as you apply and practice factor analysis," he continued.

"I am afraid I am confused about the eigenvalues," she said with annoyance; "neither do I understand what you mean by factor loadings,"

He pondered and said, "The factor loadings indicate the strength of the correlations between each variable and its factor."

"I hope this is helpful," he added instantly.

After Energia had heard his clarification, she was amazed, and she exclaimed, "Factor analysis is quite sophisticated and impressive!"

"Yes, it is indeed," he agreed enthusiastically.

After spending several hours listening to her advisor's perspectives on correlation analysis, regression analysis, time-series analysis, and factor analysis, Energia rushed into a quiet computer lab across.

Puzzled by her move, Chercheur got worried. "What explains that rush?" he asked, uttering concerns about her. "I hope everything is fine."

"There is nothing to worry about, I am fine and I have everything under control," she answered metaphorically.

She went into the computer lab carrying a set of data she had obtained from Mr. Sun's office in Sun City. She also carried data she had collected from Choice City and Wind City. This made Chercheur guess she intended to analyze some data, and he was not wrong.

Inside the computer lab, Energia sat down comfortably before a computer located in a remote corner of the room. She opened a computer program called SPSS (which means Statistical Package for the Social Sciences) to perform a battery of tests on her data.

Chercheur had introduced her to SPSS as a standard integrated system of computer tests for data analysis.

She was fond of SPSS for a few specific reasons. She appreciated the impressive number of tests it offered for statistical analysis, including t-test for independent groups, paired-samples t-test, one-way analysis of variance, correlation analysis, regression analysis, factor analysis, and many other tests. She also enjoyed its flexible data format. She found it helpful how SPSS provided its users with the options of a *Windows method* and a *syntax method*. The *Windows method* would take its users through the clicks of windows and dialog boxes to select the tests and variables relevant to the analysis. The *syntax method* would require its users to learn and demonstrate proficiency in the language of formulas used to implement statistical analyses.

Though Chercheur had warned Energia that both methods presented some advantages and disadvantages, she felt more comfortable with the *Windows method*, because she found it easy to use, following much practice or lab trials, and after mulling over her choice.

"The *Windows method* feels like a fun game that takes you from one click to another one, you just need to know the next step and its meaning," she once confided to her advisor.

Concentrating on her data in front of the computer, Energia identified three variables of interest for her analysis. The three variables were *solar energy use*, *air quality*, and *water quality*.

She set to examine the correlation between solar energy use and air pollution in Sun City by analyzing the data she had obtained from the office of the Mayor of Sun City, Mr. Sun.

As she prepared to set up a data file using the Windows method in SPSS, she created a codebook with the names of her variables and their coding descriptions on a scratch paper. She would use that information to define her variables in the *Variable View* icon of SPSS, by specifying their names, their labels, their values (if necessary), and their levels of measurement as nominal, ordinal, or interval-ratio.

After defining her variables, she clicked on the *Data View* icon of SPSS to enter her data.

Next, she would test the basic assumptions of linearity and homoscedasticity to make sure correlation analysis would be an appropriate test in this case. The assumption of linearity would imply that the relationship between the two variables of *solar energy use* and *air quality* could represent a straight line. The assumption of homoscedasticity would mean that changes in the scores of *air quality* were consistent with changes in the scores of *solar energy use.*

To that end, from the menu bar of her SPSS, Energia clicked on *Graphs*, then *Scatter/Dot*, and she selected the *Simple Scatter* icon. Following SPSS, step by step, she clicked on the *Define* icon to open the *Simple Scatterplot* window. In the open window, she transferred the variable of solar energy use to the Y axis and the variable of air quality to the X axis. She would also click on the *Options* icon in the open window to select the option of *excluding cases listwise* to handle missing values.

She would click on the *Continue* icon to go back to the *Simple Scatterplot* window. There, she clicked on the *OK* icon to run the analysis of testing the assumptions on linearity and homoscedasticity.

The results of the analysis presented a scatterplot that confirmed a linear relationship between the variables of *solar energy use* and *air quality*. As the scores of *solar energy use* increased, so did the scores of *air quality*. The scatterplot obtained also showed the assumption of homoscedasticity was met. Changes in the scores of *air quality* remained relatively constant from one score to another score of *solar energy use.*

Happy with the outcome of that first step, Energia felt confident to run a correlation analysis.

From the menu bar, she would click on the *Analyze* icon. From the long list of tests, she would select *Correlate*, then *Bivariate Correlations*. Once the window of Bivariate Correlations opened, she ensured the boxes of both the *Pearson correlation coefficient* and the *two-tailed test of significance* were checked. There, she transferred the two variables of solar energy use and air quality to the *Variables* field. She also clicked the *Options* icon to ensure the field of *Exclude cases pairwise* was checked for handling missing values. Next, she clicked on the *Continue* icon to return to the *Bivariate Correlations* window where she would click the *OK* icon to complete the analysis.

The results displayed in the SPSS output confirmed a positive and statistically significant correlation between *solar energy use* and *air quality* over a period of ten years in Sun City. The *Pearson correlation coefficient (r)* stood at 0.895. This meant that as the scores of *solar energy use* increased, so did the scores of *air quality*. The results implied that the use of solar energy significantly contributed to reducing air pollution and increasing the chances of respiratory health in Sun City over the past ten years. The more consistently the city implemented its policies on the use of solar panels, the more its citizens enjoyed good air quality.

Thrilled by these results, Energia seized the same opportunity to examine the correlation between the two variables of *solar energy use* and *water quality* in Sun City. The results of her *Spearman correlation analysis* showed a positive and statistically significant correlation between *solar energy use* and *water quality* over a period of ten years in Sun City. The *Spearman correlation coefficient* (rho) was 0.853. This meant that as the scores of *solar energy use* increased, so did those of *water quality*. The results implied that the use of solar panels contributed to significant reductions in water pollution in Sun City over the past ten years.

These results reminded Energia of some happy encounters in Sun City. While she was there for data collection, she encountered citizens of Sun City who were proud of living in a city with drinking water free of lead. During her stay in Sun City there was no known risks of lead contamination. She also remembered some history in the legislature of the city. At some point in the history of Sun City, the city council, mindful of the potentials of their territory in oil and natural gas, had put in place a solid legislation to forbid any practice of or inclination to fracking or hydrocracking in Sun City, to prevent the pollution of its surface and groundwater and the displacement of wildlife.

Using correlation analysis, she went on to examine the relationship between the two variables of *hydrocarbon fuels* and *water pollution* in Energium. She would find a positive and statistically significant correlation between those two variables. She uncovered that burning fossil fuels contributed to lead contamination, to some degree, in some neighborhoods of the kingdom of Energium where fracking and oil cracking were heavy practices.

Encouraged by the findings, and with her face lit up, Energia decided to take a step further in her analysis. Using regression analysis, she would examine how to predict the scores of *air quality* from knowing the scores of *solar energy use* by relying on the same data from Sun City.

Hooked on SPSS, she clicked on the *Analyze* icon from the menu bar. From the drop-down list, she clicked on *Regression*, and she selected *Linear Regression*.

In the *Linear Regression* window, she clicked on the *air quality* variable to transfer it to the *Dependent field*. She would also transfer the variable of *solar energy use* to the *Independent field*. In the drop-down list of the *Method field*, she selected *Enter* as the method of entry of *solar energy use*, the predicting variable.

She also clicked on the *Statistics* icon. The statistics window opened, and she checked the fields for *Estimates, Confidence intervals,* and *Model fit* to obtain the statistics required for that analysis.

Next, she clicked the *Continue* icon to return to the *Linear Regression* window. There, she would click on the *Options* icon to make sure that the fields of *Use probability of F* and *Include constant in equation* were checked.

Here again, she would click the *Continue* icon to go back to *Linear Regression* window.

In the *Linear Regression* window, she clicked the *OK* icon to complete the analysis. The SPSS output displayed results showing the *R-square* (the strength of the regression or prediction) as 0.760. It meant that the variable of *solar energy use* had explained 76% of the change observed in the variable of *air quality* in Sun City over the past ten years.

Energia could not believe her eyes, she thought those results were very significant; they confirmed that the clean air citizens of Sun City enjoyed much depended on solar energy use to a large extent, for up to seventy-six percent.

The results contrasted and challenged policymaking in the kingdom of Energium which relied heavily on hydrocarbon fuel for energy production and consumption.

Driven by the results, and aware of the potentials of Energium in offshore and onshore wind, Energia used regression analysis to predict that the exploitation of its wind potentials alone would allow the kingdom to achieve energy security maximally. If Energium were to depend mainly on its abundant wind resource, the kingdom would cut down its greenhouse gas emissions drastically, and this would result into improving the air quality for its citizens. Per the results of Energia's regression analysis, wind energy stood as a healthier alternative to oil, gas, and coal for power generation in the kingdom of Energium.

She was still contemplating the results of the regression analysis when Chercheur stopped by the computer lab on his way to the cafeteria. He wanted to check on Energia, out of curiosity, after so many hours; it was past lunchtime.

"You may want to take a break for lunch," he advised unexpectedly.

"I do not think so, I still have a long way to go, Sir!" she answered, surprised by his sudden appearance in the lab.

Obviously, Energia was fond of her data analyses.

"But I would appreciate if you could bring me a bottle of water with some light snack," she went on gently.

"I would love to," he answered politely, "unfortunately, the policies of this lab do not allow it."

"What do you mean?" she asked, staring at her advisor in amazement.

"Look!" he exclaimed, pointing to a notice by the entrance of the lab. It read: "No food or drink is allowed in this lab!"

"Why such a harsh policy?" she asked in a plaintive tone and strain.

With a reassuring voice tone, Chercheur said, "I think the intention behind the policy is positive; it is to prevent distractions, so that the users of this lab concentrate on their research; food and drink could distract at times."

"What if I am very hungry while using the lab?" she continued.

"In that case, your body whispers you need a lunch break," he said softly. "When your body speaks, it is in your interest to listen; your health, productivity, effectiveness, and success all depend on it. You deserve a break after working hard all morning; you need to stop for a moment to go eat."

Chercheur's words inspired Energia, she understood she needed a break, and she said to him, "I agree with you."

Any observer could tell by Energia's body language that it was a difficult decision for her; the bystander could easily observe that she took Chercheur's advice seriously but not literally.

Yet she decided to take a break. She saved her document on a USB flash drive and shut down her computer, before exiting the lab reluctantly.

Dragging her feet, she followed her mentor to the cafeteria for what she had anticipated to be a quick lunch break.

Inside the cafeteria she quickly grabbed a plate and put on it some salad, mashed potatoes, and a salmon steak.

As she looked around to find a table to sit, she noticed her high school friend, named Oxwe.

He had volunteered to partake in Energia's experiments in Choice City. He was excited to meet Energia in the cafeteria.

"What is new about your research? Fill me in," he said delightfully.

"I am currently analyzing the data," she replied concisely.

"Good for you!" he continued ardently.

"Let me know if I could help, I still possess a residue of skills in quantitative analysis," he added humbly.

Oxwe was the Chief Information Officer (CIO) for a major and famous multinational corporation, headquartered in the kingdom of Energium. In his capacity as a distinguished patron of data processing for the organization, he had a wealth of knowledge and experience in data analysis, and he was very proficient in running and interpreting quantitative data. He was a young, self-motivated, and successful chief information officer.

Energia's initial answer to his request was, "That is awesome to hear and know."

"Please tell me about it!" she exclaimed with admiration on a second thought.

"For your type of research," Oxwe said eagerly, "correlation analysis, regression analysis, and factor analysis would all be helpful tests to run your data."

"You read my mind, that is exactly what I am doing," she answered, mesmerized.

Before he could elaborate further, she interrupted, "I need to go now; it is nice to see you again, I will catch up with you soon, my friend."

While she was still speaking, Oxwe rushed to go get some fruit salad and cake.

He presented them to his friend and said, "Remember to enjoy some fruit and dessert before you head back, my experience in data analysis has taught me some good lessons. Your brain will need these ingredients for a balanced sugar level; data analysis can be very consuming physically, mentally, and emotionally."

Oxwe's words made Energia reminisce Chercheur's most recent advice.

"Thank you, my good friend, for your kindness and wise suggestions." she said calmly.

She took the plate of fruit salad and cake from Oxwe and sat down for a few more minutes to enjoy her food.

In the end, she felt really good about the decision to take a break for lunch, and she was very grateful to Chercheur, as she thought to herself: "*It certainly helps to trust your advisor; soon or later there are benefits to listening to and following a good mentor's golden advice.*"

Her lunch boosted her energy genuinely. The good hormones from the positive energy contaminated her often labile mood, and she suddenly felt relaxed and happy.

She felt refreshed and rejuvenated when she returned to the lab.

Back in the lab, she was eager to continue her data analysis with time-series analysis and factor analysis to run her raw data.

By relying on the data she had recorded in her journal, Energia would use time-series analysis to find that her ancestors' generation had enjoyed a cleaner air than her generation, because they had heavily depended on solar energy, wind energy, and water energy. The results of the analysis allowed her to forecast the future in terms of the long-term trends in renewable energy use. These results confirmed the previous results of her regression analysis that the rates of air pollution would decrease significantly in Energium if the kingdom shifted from hydrocarbon fuels to wind and solar energy production.

Soon after, Energia decided to utilize factor analysis to run the set of data she had collected previously in Water City, to identify the main factors contributing to global warming and climate change.

She had recorded as many as fifty variables to explain global warming and climate change. The long list of variables included gas emissions from cars, emissions from planes, industrial emissions, plastic removals, poor garbage dumping, wildfires, pesticides, agriculture, chemical wastes from pharmaceutical laboratories and hospitals, chemical leakages or spills, fracking and oil extraction and production processes, gas stations, burning gasoline, oil spills, coal plants, nuclear plants, wars, atomic explosions, deforestation, and non-human activities, to name a few.

She thought the list was way too long, and some of the variables seemed redundant. Rather than going by that long list of variables, she chose to follow a different line of reasoning, and she hypothesized that a small number of factors would explain global warming and climate change.

While reading through the long list of variables, using techniques of factor analysis, she would identify five common denominators or factors. The five factors were: (1) *greenhouse gases*, (2) *other gases and hazardous substances such as mercury and arsenic*, (3) *deforestation*, (4) *other human activities*, and (5) *non-human activities such as naturally-occurring radioactivity*. She reduced the long list by regrouping its variables in five groups of ten variables (around the five factors identified).

She would employ factor analysis to examine whether and how the fifty variables reflected the five factors she had identified. Step by step, she would apply the *Windows method* of SPSS for data entry and analysis.

From the menu bar, she clicked the *Analyze* icon. From the drop-down list, she selected the *Data Reduction* icon and chose the *Factor Analysis* test. The *Factor Analysis* window opened, and she highlighted the fifty variables and transferred them to the *Variables* field.

She clicked the *Descriptives'* icon to acquire a *correlation matrix* with enough correlations to justify the use of factor analysis as a test in that situation.

In the open *Descriptives'* window, she ensured the field of *Initial solution* was checked by default, and she also checked the fields of *Coefficients* and *KMO and Bartlett's test of sphericity*.

She would next click the *Continue* icon to return to the *Factor Analysis* window.

In the open *Factor Analysis* window, she clicked the *Extraction* icon. When the *Extraction* window opened, she selected the *Principal components* from the drop-down list as the extraction method. She also ensured the default value was 1 in the field of *Eigenvalues over*. Next, she checked the

Scree plot field to get a *Scree plot* of the number of factors extracted, and she clicked the *Continue* icon to go back to the *Factor Analysis* window.

In the open *Factor Analysis* window, she would click the *Rotation* icon. In the open *Rotation* window, she checked the *Varimax* field to request a *Varimax* rotation for the extracted factors. Then, she clicked the *Continue* icon to return to the *Factor Analysis* window.

In the open *Factor Analysis* window, she clicked the *Options'* icon. In the open *Options'* window, she selected the field of *Exclude cases pairwise* to exclude any variable with a missing value from the factor analysis. She also checked the *Sorted by size* field to rank the factor loadings from the largest to the smallest in the SPSS output. Additionally, she checked the field of *Suppress absolute values less than* and typed the value of 0.33 in the empty field to request the suppression of factor loadings with smaller values than 0.33 in the SPSS output. Her goal here was to retain only factor loadings that accounted for at least ten percent of the change in their factor for significance.

Next, she would click the *Continue* icon to go back to the *Factor Analysis* window. In the open Factor Analysis window, she clicked the *OK* icon to finalize the analysis.

The SPSS output presented the results of the factor analysis in the forms of a *Correlation Matrix* table, a *KMO and Bartlett's test* table, a table of *Communalities*, a table of the *Total Variance Explained*, a *Component Matrix table*, a *Rotated Component Matrix table*, and a table of *Component Transformation Matrix*.

The *Correlation Matrix* table showed high correlations among the fifty variables. The inter-correlations between gas emissions from cars, emissions from planes, industrial emissions, wildfires, chemical leaks or spills, gas stations, burning gasoline, oil spills, and mining were higher than 0.33 in magnitude. It meant that the choice of factor analysis as a test was a good one for that case. The table of the *Bartlett's test of sphericity* also confirmed factor analysis as the correct choice of test.

The *Communalities* table reflected the proportion of change the common factors accounted for in each variable, by using the principal components analysis as the method for extracting the factors.

The table of the *Total Variance Explained* showed five common factors, with their respective eigenvalues. It also displayed the percentage of total variance and the cumulative percentage of total variance each of the factors accounted for. The analysis retained the five factors (*greenhouse gases, other gases and hazardous substances, deforestation, other human activities*, and *non-human activities*) that displayed eigenvalues of 1 or higher. The factor of the *greenhouse gases* accounted for thirty-five percent of the global warming and climate change; the factor of the *other gases* explained global warming and climate change by nineteen percent; the factor of *deforestation* accounted for global warming and climate change by eighteen percent; the factor of *other human activities* explained global warming and climate change by fifteen percent; the factor of *non-human activities* accounted for global warming and climate change by ten percent. It meant that the five factors explained ninety-seven percent of the total variance, which is significant and impressive.

The table of the *Component Matrix* presented the five factors extracted with specific correlation coefficients or factor loadings reflecting the correlations between the five factors and the fifty variables respectively. The factors the *Component Matrix* presented were not rotated, meaning their extraction was performed based on the percentage of the overall change (or total variance) explained. Energia noticed that the absence of rotation coincided with significant cross-loadings, showing some variables loaded highly on multiple factors, which would make it difficult to interpret the factors for meaning.

The table of the *Rotated Component Matrix* displayed the five factors extracted with *Varimax* rotation. There, the factor loadings indicated that forty of the fifty variables loaded highly on the five factors of (*greenhouse gases, other gases and hazardous substances, deforestation, other human activities*, and *non-human activities*). Ten variables cross-loaded significantly across multiple factors.

To make the interpretation of the results of her factor analysis easier, Energia would delete the ten cross-loaded variables. In the end, the results confirmed her initial hypothesis that a small number of factors explained global warming and climate change. Making due allowances, she utilized factor analysis successfully to reduce a long list of fifty variables to identify five factors contributing to global warming and climate change. Per the results of her analysis, the five factors encompassed *greenhouse gases, other gases and hazardous substances, deforestation, other human activities*, and *non-human activities*.

Thrilled with the results and the line of reasoning, Energia was amazed by the technical ability of factor analysis to simplify or reduce data.

Mesmerized by these meaningful results, she kept staring so intently into the SPSS output on her computer, when Chercheur appeared suddenly from nowhere and asked, "How far are you?"

Her answer was spontaneous, "I just finished," she said while jumping for joy, "and the results are quite significant."

"Come and see," she added, inviting her advisor to draw near the computer screen.

He checked the results carefully and exclaimed enthusiastically, "Scientific methods are interestingly beautiful and relevant to knowledge and progress!"

"What do you think of such magnificent results?" he went on softly.

"I still can't believe my eyes, but I did it," she said promptly.

"Congratulations!" he replied.

"What do the results tell you? What do they imply overall?" he added curiously.

"I think the message is clear, if we promote renewable energy use, we will be able to mitigate or curb greenhouse gas emissions and boost our chances to be healthy and save our planet," she answered smoothly.

"Well said and well done," Chercheur responded before exiting the room to head home for dinner with his family.

Energia was bidding him goodbye when the alarm on his phone sounded suddenly and quite loudly.

"Is everything fine?" she asked, worried.

"Do not worry, this is to remind me it is time to go home for dinner. If you want to know more about it, go check with my wife and daughter," he said, trying to rush out.

Energia giggled and said while nodding, "I understand, Ms. Luz has the appropriate toolbox for good and helpful ground rules. You better hurry up!"

Not long after Chercheur's departure, she rearranged her papers, saved her files, and shut down her computer before leaving. She was apparently happy and satisfied with what she had achieved in terms of her data analyses and the outstanding results.

CHAPTER 6

Strengths and Limitations of Results and Implications for Policymaking

Two weeks later, Energia would throw a memorable party to celebrate the results of her research. She invited many of her friends, including Oxwe and other lifelong friends.

At the outset of the event, an argument broke among her friends as to which method was the best for conducting research. Oxwe was certainly aware this was the sixty-four-thousand-dollar question, yet he decided to put the question to Energia, to embarrass or trap her. "Tell us briefly," he said cleverly, "which is the finest, the greatest, or the most efficient method for doing research?"

"You ask the million-dollar question," she confessed humbly. "I'm afraid I don't know." Unable to solve the dilemma due to her personal biases, Energia motioned to her advisor for help. Chercheur's solution was simple, and it caught them all by surprise. "Neither of the methods is best," he explained. "Each method has its weaknesses adjacent to its strengths. Depending on the research topics and what the researchers want to achieve, they select a method or the methods that meet the needs of their research and suit its goals."

He would use that venue skillfully to challenge Energia on the limitations of her research.

At every step of the research process, Chercheur had alerted Energia on being mindful of the weak or shaky aspects of her research. Immediately prior to the stage of data analysis, he had warned her over this through an insightful lecture:

"Listen!" he said to Energia. "Every scientific or human method has its strengths and limitations. In scientific investigations, the traditional ninety-five percent confidence level, as reflected purposely in the SPSS outputs from data analyses, implies the need for humility in navigating research and science. This is a reminder that the processes and outcomes of scientific inquiries are not perfect, and they can never be perfect. The results of scientific investigations cannot pretend to be effective at a hundred percent."

"Research teaches us to be humble," he went on modestly. "It unveils to us the limitations in what we know and our shortcomings in what we do not know. It reminds us there is a lot we do not know; a lot remains inaccessible to our understanding, much more still needs to be discovered. In the final analysis, we become mindful that even the small drop we think we know could still defy us, for it hides or conceals random aspects we are not aware of. Some dimensions of reality will keep challenging our understanding relentlessly."

"The multiple pathways to scientific discoveries are paved with threats to reliability and validity," he persisted convincingly. "Per my modest experience, there always is a margin of error; there is always some room for improvement in research and science. That is why no Covid-19 vaccine is effective at one hundred percent. That is why every medication or remedy has its side effects. That is also why no energy source is perfect. Non-renewable energies and renewable energies all bear shortcomings or pitfalls. Every human achievement or discovery comes with its flaws or inadequacies, because the humankind is full of existential imperfections.

Every researcher needs to be mindful of the limitations of the process and outcome of their research. I hope you remain aware of the deficiencies in your research; I hope and pray you are able to identify the shaky sides of your investigations or the weak links in their processes and outcomes."

Energia had understood Chercheur's warning at the onset of her research, and she had cherished his advice throughout. Aware of the limitations or insufficiencies in each research methodology, she felt the need to complement the lack of magnitude in qualitative interviews and observations with the large scope of quantitative surveys. She would compensate the defects of rigor in surveys with the rigor of experiments. In the end, she would adopt and advocate for mixed methods to boost reliability and validity in research in the social sciences.

In the same perspective, Energia became mindful that every type of energy had its advantages and disadvantages.

Chercheur saw in the celebration of the results a timely opportunity to call out Energia on the limitations of her research.

He started by pointing to specific shortages in Energia's research methods.

"Young lady!" he exclaimed. "It seems you are fond of the number 'one hundred'. In the process of your research, you had often limited your sample sizes to *one hundred* for your surveys. A sample of *one hundred* is certainly good in quantitative research, but a sample of five hundred cases or one thousand participants would be even more representative. The bigger or larger is the sample size, the more significant it is with regard to reliability and validity, and the more relevant it becomes to policymaking."

Energia was all ears, while Chercheur kept on talking.

He stared at her suddenly and said with a smile, "After all those long months of tireless investigations, with enlightened data collections and analyses, what can you tell us about the limitations of solar energy?"

Her answer would not disappoint him, she would come out strongly to make her case in front of the large cohort of friends.

"It is interesting you ask that question," she replied politely. "There is no doubt, solar energy is not a perfect recipe for the issues of global warming and climate change."

"Tell us more about that," Oxwe interrupted eagerly.

Energia said, "Per the findings of my data collection in Sun City, solar energy was definitely inexpensive in the long run, but the initial costs of the installation of solar panels and solar lightning were relatively high according to the citizens of Sun City. Citizens of Sun City had indicated that the batteries could also be expensive and contribute to some level of contamination. Moreover, the data from Sun City revealed that the processes of manufacturing the solar panels contributed to some level of greenhouse gas emissions.

"Some citizens of Sun City confided that the solar panels were invasive of their space. The solar collectors or devices could occupy or spread over large spaces, they would take up much of your space. The solar plants in Sun City spread over vast expanses of lands, cleaned of green forests. Other citizens confessed the solar energy was intermittent, depending on the weather and the period of the year; some users could not harness solar energy in the winter months or on cloudy or stormy days.

"Let me make it clear, if the country or city you reside in enjoys the sunshine most of the year, your solar panels would cover your needs in energy consistently throughout the year. However, if you live in a region where the sunshine is sporadic, the solar panels might not help you meet all your needs in energy."

Her answer left Chercheur in complete awe.

"What a great performance, Energia!" he said with reverential respect. "Your response is impressive."

"How about the limitations of hydroelectric power?" he wondered subsequently.

Without beating around the bush, she replied head-on, "In accordance with the data I collected from Water City, water energy was undeniably cheap in the long run, but the dams were expensive to build at the outset. Some citizens of Water City complained how salmon was a rare commodity in their city; the presence of dams obstructed or affected negatively the life and the reproduction cycle of fish such as salmon. In Water City, I learned that the construction and operation of the dams could lead to the destruction of wildlife habitat and the displacement of the local population in some cases. Many citizens expressed anger at the fact the sustained construction and maintenance of dams fostered the destruction of wildlife habitat in Water City.

"Moreover, the water reservoirs could contribute to droughts, per the data collected in Water City. The decomposition of the plants resting at the bottom of those reservoirs contributed to some levels of carbon dioxide and methane emissions, according to the data I collected from city officials. Furthermore, citizens complained the dams had extended over enormous spaces and deprived the farmers of acres of fertile or arable land they could plough and cultivate for profitable agriculture.

"Finally, as you all know, hydraulic energy relies on the movements of water and the levels of precipitation. Therefore, it would be quite imperative and wise to conduct some field and need analyses prior to adopting hydropower. If your country or city abounds in water or enjoys high levels of precipitation all over the year, you can be sure to rest on consistent or stable hydroelectric energy. But if you live in a region where water is rare, it may be difficult to rely on hydropower for all your needs in energy."

Again, Energia's balanced perspectives left her advisor wonderstruck.

"Good job!" he exclaimed.

"What about the limitations of wind energy?" he added, while motioning to Energia to keep up the good work.

She took a deep breath and said, "Per my data collection in Wind City, just like solar energy, wind energy is intermittent. Your country or city may want to do a field analysis before adopting that type of energy. If you live in coastal regions, or if you are on high elevations and enjoy strong or speedy winds throughout the year, your wind energy will be consistent.

"While listening to the city officials of Wind City, I learned that the production and installation of their wind turbines were costly, though there was evidence that wind energy was low-cost compared to hydrocarbon fuels. Some citizens of Wind City complained the turbines had fostered noise pollution, and their operation contributed to low visibility in some areas of the city. Other citizens indicated that the wind turbines had contributed to the migration of birds; it was obvious that the blades of the turbines posed a serious threat to birds and wildlife. Wind City had reported high numbers in bird deaths due its wind turbines; during my stay in Wind City I once witnessed the blades strike two birds fatally. The city council's initiatives in promoting the design and production of bladeless wind turbines had helped tremendously on that account.

"Citizens also complained the wind farms were too expansive. Their installations in Wind City took up large acreages, which was detrimental to traditional farming."

"Well done, once again!" Chercheur said excitedly. "Now tell me, what has your research identified as the limitations of electric vehicles?"

Energia paused, grabbed a bottle of water, and sipped some water before she continued, glancing at her watch.

"Listen, due to their zero direct emission, electric vehicles tend to be less damaging to the environment than conventional vehicles, per my data collection. But the data revealed that electric vehicles could also pose some threats to environmental health. My data analysis showed that, depending on their sources of energy, they could contribute to drastic increases in greenhouse emissions. Electric vehicles relying on the coal or other fossil fuels as their sources of electricity would escalate carbon emissions and toxic pollution in the atmosphere. To be specific, there would not be any benefits to the environment in advocating for electric vehicles in countries like Energium where the fossil fuels represent the mainstream source of electric power, except the kingdom first shifts from hydrocarbon fuels to renewable energy sources. Per the results of my data analysis, electric vehicles that run on renewable energies are less polluting and more beneficial to the environment."

"Also be mindful," she continued majestically, "the factories producing electric vehicles and their batteries in the Kingdom of Energium release much toxic waste because of their high demands in copper, aluminum, nickel, and other toxic minerals. The fumes from the batteries could harm the human health and the environment."

After a brief moment of silence to give a thought to her next words, she went on reluctantly, "Honestly, in view of their limitations, I am concerned and worried that electric vehicles in the long run might be counterproductive to our efforts in curbing global warming; they may hamper our progress in or chances of mitigating climate change. Personally, as crazy as this may seem to some of you, I would prefer a horse-drawn carriage or coach of the olden days to an electric vehicle, in my attempt at saving our planet. Of course, you can disagree with me on this option. I understand some of you may find that my choice is cruel to the horses.

But I opt for a logic of cost-benefit analysis to maximize our chances of reducing greenhouse gas emissions."

"Wow!" Oxwe interrupted. "What are brilliant idea of going back to the carriage rides in this context, I love it!"

"Yes, indeed. I endorse that wonderful idea," said Chercheur.

"Please tell me, per your research, is there anything wrong about using paper bags or brown bags?" he continued, with a look yearning for a glimpse of scientific answer from his advisee.

Apparently exhausted, Energia yawned, stretched her arms and said, "Some use of paper bags or brown bags in our grocery stores would do less harm than the mainstream usage of plastic bags across Energium. The paper bags present the risk of killing our trees and wiping out our forests. But we can counter that risk by planting new young trees before using the old ones for making bags or furniture, or for building houses. Paper bags are healthier for the environment than plastic bags; the benefits of using paper bags are higher for our health than their costs."

"Ironically," Chercheur interrupted, "your data had displayed the pace or rate of deforestation to be higher than that of reforestation in Energium."

"Shame on us in the Kingdom of Energium!" Energia replied abruptly. "We should be planting more trees than we destroy and consume."

"Well, help may be on the way or just around the corner! Under your leadership, we could be planting more trees in the coming months," Chercheur said, as a compliment to Energia.

"Certainly," Oxwe concurred with a smile.

Energia giggled and said humbly, "I hope so, it depends on all of us to lend a hand."

"Absolutely!" exclaimed Chercheur with a round of loud applauses to congratulate his mentee.

The audience joined him in a standing ovation to praise Energia's exceptional performance.

"I appreciate all your compliments," Energia interrupted. "Let us now spice up the party by moving to the rhythm of music; it is fair to be glad and rejoice together at this moment, we deserve to celebrate and enjoy every minute of this unique occasion."

She rushed to her computer and selected her favorite playlist of songs. The playlist displayed a variety of genres to all the guests' taste and satisfaction. Everyone enjoyed listening to the music and dancing to the nice beats. The guests would take turns at the podium to show their moves. Oxwe's moves were the most impressive. His performance revealed some great dance skills. He truly electrified the crowd with his body moves. His moves wowed every guest, and as he kept dancing tirelessly, the audience cheered from the sidelines.

Energia was awestruck by his moves, and she could not help but say to him, "I did not know you as a dancer, you are such a talented dancer!"

"I appreciate the compliment, it makes my day," replied Oxwe with smiling face.

The event made everyone happy that evening. It was a joyful gathering; the party was a great venue for celebration and networking.

At the end of the party, all the guests expressed their gratitude to Energia for organizing and hosting such a convivial gathering. They also praised her for the results of her research, before vacating her house.

Interestingly and spontaneously, Oxwe volunteered to help Energia clean up the mess. He quickly collected the trash from the floor and tables, by removing the dirty napkins hanging around, the used paper plates and cups, and the used wooden forks and spoons. He carefully put them all in large paper bags and placed them by the front door, for the municipal garbage collection. He also cleared the empty paper bottles or containers for recycling, before bidding goodbye to his host.

Energia marveled at his act of kindness, and she appreciated it by saying to him, "Thank you, for being such a gentleman! You made this evening special. I hope to see you again."

"Certainly," Oxwe answered gallantly, as he crossed the exit.

Before leaving, Chercheur whispered in Energia's ears some motivational words: "Please do not stop here," he ordered, "this is not the end of your journey, it is the beginning; the next step is even more relevant, remember to make your research useful to policymaking. In doing so, you could help transform our society for the better."

"Sure, Sir, I promise! You can count on my goodwill," she replied gratefully.

A few months later, upon Chercheur's insistence to make her findings accessible to policymakers, Energia published the results of her research in a very popular peer-reviewed journal of the Kingdom of Energium.

In parallel with the publication, she would submit a policy proposal on wind energy to the energy department of her country. Simultaneously, she submitted a grant proposal to a philanthropic foundation set by a generous private citizen to support clean energy initiatives; she applied for a total of four hundred million dollars to promote solar panels in local communities across the Kingdom of Energium.

The application was successful, and she got the impressive grant. She would manage the money professionally and with accountability. She would use her hometown of Djehon as the site for a pilot program. In the implementation process she worked closely in consultation with the city officials and local authorities. She randomly selected one thousand households from fifty neighborhoods that had volunteered to partake in the experiment. This was not only an experiment, but it was like an action research driven by the participants and aimed at bringing tangible, factual, practical, and sustainable changes to their hometown. Mindful of Chercheur's previous advice on the value of a large sample size, she selected a sample of one thousand houses, for reliability, validity, and significance in policymaking.

She used a colossal amount of the money to top the one thousand houses with solar panels. The installations of the solar panels were very expensive and expansive; it was quite an ambitious undertaking and a costly operation. Every household also got enough money to maintain their solar panels and pay their electric bills for the duration of the experiment over a period of twelve months. Besides, she used part of the grant to buy out the cars belonging to the one thousand households participating in the action research. In return, each participant in the study received a bicycle and a horse as their new means of transportation.

She also used some money from the grant to purchase young plants to organize weekly campaigns of reforestation in Djehon. Every Saturday, she mobilized the participants in the study to plant new young trees around the streets and public places in the city over a period of a year. Some of the grant served to feed the participants during the reforestation campaigns. Each participant would receive a financial incentive for planting at least a young tree by the end of every weekend.

A year later, all the participants in the study reported a reduction in their stress level for riding bicycles or horses as their means of transportation instead of cars. Many residents reported they felt a difference in the quality of air in the environment. Djehon recorded a drastic drop in air pollution in that period. The rates of car accidents and traffic-related fatalities plummeted in the town. The news quickly spread around the city and across Energium, as the participants in the study shared it with family members, relatives, and friends. Energia would make the headlines of major newspapers in the kingdom. She was the guest of many news channels. She appeared on several shows on the radio and television. She did not hesitate to use her numerous appearances to promote her project and ideas on renewable energy.

With a high volume of additional financial support from local businesses highly fascinated and interested in the manifest results, a program that had started discreetly in her hometown culminated in a megaproject, with a litany of successful replications in other neighboring towns and local communities across the Kingdom of Energium.

In view of the encouraging impacts of the program on the city of Djehon and its positive ripple effects in the region, the mayor and the city council formally and successfully endorsed the program as a public policy for the entire city. This move was welcomed greatly and widely, to all the citizens' satisfaction. The decision galvanized and empowered Energia. She would commit fully to scale up the implementation process to cover every household in her hometown. After only a few months, the city of Djehon became famous for its bicycle rides and horse rides. Notably, three international organizations recognized the city as one of the healthiest places to live on earth. Alongside the recognitions, Djehon won a prestigious clean energy price as the cleanest city in Energium. Mindful of those facts, the department of energy officially recognized Djehon as the cleanest and healthiest city of the Kingdom of Energium.

Just then Energia got some good news from the department of energy. Following a thorough review of her policy proposal and after several months of deliberations, the department contacted and hired Energia to oversee a pilot program for the exploitation of Energium's offshore and onshore wind for energy production. She gladly accepted the offer. She would use her first days in the position to assemble immediately a diverse and competent team tasked with diagnosing the issues and assessing the needs, designing a specific system for addressing the issues, implementing, and evaluating the system on the micro and macro levels in Energium.

After nearly two years of coordinated field research, involving carefully conducted diagnoses in local communities, persistent assessments of local capacities, and strategic assets and needs analyses, Energia launched and oversaw a vast multilayered operation for developing wind farms across the Kingdom of Energium, mainly in the regions of high elevations and in coastal areas or cities where the wind would be abundant, strong, and consistent throughout the calendar year. The energy department set a multibillion-dollar budget to establish and run wind power stations for supplying the kingdom with renewable energy solutions.

Strategically paced over three years, the implementation would result in the installations of two hundred wind power plants to generate electricity in Energium. The two hundred wind parks were equipped with highly efficient bladeless wind turbines. Energia had opted for the technology of bladeless turbines to minimize the risk of bird fatalities. She would confide to the workers in the factories producing the wind turbines, pleading: "I love the birds from the bottom of my heart, they inspire me as they fly, I enjoy having them around, and I would do anything to protect them. Be mindful to do whatever it takes to save their lives as you design and make the wind turbines; we all need these birds for a balanced ecosystem in Energium."

Her compassionate plea would move the factory workers deeply. Filled with sympathy for the bird population in Energium, they carefully and skillfully crafted innovative bladeless wind turbines to accommodate the presence of birds, without jeopardizing their movements.

Five years later, following a successful pilot program, the implementation of Energia's ambitious wind energy proposal would progressively shift Energium from its total dependence on hydrocarbon fuels to heavily rely on wind energy to generate electricity. In record time, citizens of Energium started feeling some immediate impacts on their health. Across the kingdom, citizens reported breathing good air; the levels of air pollution dropped drastically in many pockets of the country. Energia conducted a couple of studies that found a clear reduction in greenhouse gas emissions in the kingdom. In view of the tangible and rewarding results, the department of energy was proud of how the carbon emissions decreased quickly only after a few years of wind energy use. The country recorded some sharp declines in lung cancer, asthma, and other respiratory diseases among its citizens. Energia would disclose to some friends she felt more relaxed and happy traveling around the cities of the kingdom in that period. In a phone conversation, she would confide to Chercheur: "I am now proud to be a citizen of Energium, I am happy and healthy living in my country. Thank you!"

Needless to mention her advisor was very pleased with her achievements for the health of their nation.

Under her leadership the department of forestry would also initiate a vast and successful campaign of reforestation in every city of the Kingdom of Energium. They would provide substantial financial incentives to motivate citizens for reforestation. Local businesses supported the initiative by empowering and providing citizens with meaningful reward packages, awarding free prepaid vacations, bonuses, and gift cards. Every adult citizen happily committed to planting a tree every month in a house, in a farm, or in a public place with the smooth approval of their city.

Amid her successful professional achievements, the chances of success in Energia's relationship and private life also skyrocketed. A few weeks following the party in celebration of the results of her research, Oxwe called to check on her. The memorable evening phone call would be a game changer, the start of a romantic relationship between the two lovers. Happy evenings together and weekend dates would season and refine their relationship for the next six months.

Their first date took them to a small local restaurant in Djefon. The name of the restaurant was Ganji. It was Energia's favorite restaurant. It was also one of the local businesses that had supported the clean energy program in her hometown. The owner Mrs. Zan was a champion of green energy. All the dishes in her menu were homemade. Her team cooked the food, using a variety of freshly harvested organic vegetables and fruits from local farmers. Her popular vegetables included leaves such as kale, collard greens, spinach, green and red chard, okra, arugula, dandelion, cabbage, zucchini, cucumber, eggplant, radish, beetroot, turnip, carrot, tomato, breadfruit, beans, butternut squash, and roots such potatoes, cassava, and yam. Her most commonly served fruits included orange, apple, papaya, banana, plum, grapes, blueberries, strawberries, blackberries, mango, avocado, pineapple, kiwifruit, and watermelon. They also served rice, quinoa, couscous, and pasta, with wild-caught fish such as tilapia, porgy, salmon, tuna, cod, mahi-mahi, black bass, white bass, catfish, flounder, butterfish, trout, and rockfish. Their rice and quinoa could also come with baked chicken, omelet, scrambled egg, or boiled egg. Their seafood also included crab, shrimp, lobsters, and oysters. They mainly baked or boiled their food to their customers' taste and satisfaction. Their list of spices featured garlic, onion, ginger, turmeric, oregano, thyme, basil, rosemary, and parsley.

On that first date, Energia ordered some broiled salmon with steamed turnip greens and kale, baked potatoes, and black grapes. She loved broiled salmon so much. Oxwe settled for some baked black bass with a combination of blanched mustard greens and red chard, boiled yam, and red papaya. The food was delicious and healthy, served in wooden plates and bowls with wooden forks and spoons. The drinking water was also served in wooden cups. The couple spent their evening together happily.

Their third date was in Energia's apartment. She had offered to fix a home-cooked meal for their evening together. It was on a Saturday, and she had enough time to boil some rice, make some tomato sauce with olive oil, simmer some spinach, and bake some white bass to Oxwe's taste. Black or white bass was his favorite fish. She would also steam some beetroot with eggplant as a side dish. The fruit on her menu was watermelon.

Mindful Energia was fond of boiled black-eyed peas, Oxwe decided to surprise her by volunteering to cook some of these delicious beans.

As Oxwe put on his apron, Energia wondered, "What are you trying to do here?"

"I want to help in the kitchen," he replied swiftly.

"There is not much you can do here," she said hilariously.

"Wait until you see!" he exclaimed charmingly.

Just then Energia stepped out of the kitchen to go to the bathroom.

Oxwe seized that opportunity to put some water in a pot and set it on the stove to boil.

Before Energia could figure it out, Oxwe had rinsed some beans, emptied the dirty water in the sink, and found his way to the stove.

He dumped the beans in the boiling water and covered the pot.

It was a great surprise for Energia when she returned to the kitchen.

She noticed the black-eyed peas cooking.

"Where did you get this from?" she asked, mesmerized, pointing to the beans.

"I bought it for you," he answered politely.

"That is kind of you; black-eyed peas are one of my favorite food, and they go well with rice," she said ecstatically.

"I know something about that," he replied while giggling.

"But I did not know you were a cook!" she exclaimed, while wrapping her hands around Oxwe's head, and covering his face with gentle kisses.

"And I was not aware you were a chef," he reacted graciously.

And they both burst into laughter while hugging and kissing.

They would enjoy a delicious meal and evening together.

Their relationship would continue to improve and mature one date after another; it would reach a point where they could not spend a day without talking to one another on the phone.

After six months of delightful dating, Oxwe thought the time was ripe for them to take their relationship to the next level.

He would use a quiet weekend date in his apartment to take his chances and propose to Energia thoughtfully.

While the couple savored the delectable fish and couscous dish he fixed for the occasion, Oxwe stood up suddenly, pushed his chair to the side, and got down on his knees.

"Are you alright?" Energia asked, apparently concerned. She thought Oxwe had a malaise.

"May I ask for a favor?" he said with furtive eyes.

She did not have a clue what his intention was when she nodded and said, "Go ahead!"

"What do you want?" she continued impatiently, before Oxwe could speak.

"Would you marry me?" he asked in a shaky voice, but with a smile, by presenting Energia with a shiny ring.

She took a deep breath and said, "First, I must confess, it scared me how you went down on your knees, I was not expecting this."

She would move on to test Oxwe with a set of pertinent and defiant questions.

"Are you really sure you know what you are asking for? Are you fully aware of all the implications of your request?" she asked, obviously enthused.

"Will you accept my weaknesses or shortcomings?" she added, with her eyes tearing up.

In a splendid gesture, Oxwe grabbed some napkins and wiped her tears affectively.

"Yes, I will," he replied softly, "you can count on me in the midst of contradictions."

"Will you be there for me in times of desolation and difficulties?" she went on insistently.

"Yes, I will," he reassured her, "you can lean on me in the darkness without worrying, for I will be your stronghold. I will be the refuge you can always resort to for peace, a shelter you can dwell in safely."

"I will be there to listen to you and care for you when everybody is gone," he added elegantly.

"Can you have the patience to spend the rest of your life with me, regardless of what it takes?" she persisted assertively.

"Yes, I can. I will be there always for you as the friend you can trust day and night, your best friend, to keep you company and to protect you," he replied gracefully, still down on his knees.

"How would any lady reject a gentleman like you?" Energia went on, with tears rolling down her cheeks again, "I feel honored, and I welcome your proposal with all my heart. Yes, I will!"

Overjoyed that her new fiancé just passed the test with high marks, before Oxwe could get up, Energia stretched her arms to reach out and lift him up in a beautiful scene of hugs and kisses. She covered Oxwe's lips and cheeks with sustained kisses. The newly engaged couple's joy was incommensurable, and their happiness was evident.

A year later, the couple happily pronounced their wedding vows in front of relatives, family members, colleagues, and selected friends. In a beautiful green city garden in Djehon, and in a sober wedding ceremony, Energia and Oxwe would cordially accept to spend the rest of their lives together as wife and husband.

Through a short, allegorical, and original wedding vow, Energia said to Oxwe, staring at him, "My dear fiancé, will you accept to be my best friend at night and in broad daylight, now and always?"

By referring to "*night*" in the vow, she implied the dark, sad, or difficult moments of turbulences, contradictions, sickness, misunderstanding, conflict, crisis, or issues of any kind. The phrase "*broad daylight*" in the vow stood for moments of happiness.

"Yes, I will," he said wholeheartedly.

Using the same formula, Oxwe made a similar request to Energia, and she responded positively and unreservedly.

The two spouses would share sustained intimate kisses for nearly three minutes.

The memorable scene occurred in the presence of a supportive crowd of jubilant eyewitnesses, and with blessings from a religious leader by the name of Abab.

After the new spouses had completed making their vow, a wedding reception followed immediately. A classy team of chefs from Mrs. Zan's popular restaurant Ganji cooked the food. Mrs. Zan dispatched a group of caring waiters and waitresses to serve the meal. The food was delicious and healthy. The guests would all enjoy it. They were happy to have their meals served in wooden plates; they were pleased to eat with wooden forks, spoons, and knives.

One guest, Miss Yema, Energia's friend and bridesmaid would confide to the bride, "I was not aware there were wooden plates and knives available on the market; they are very good and easy to use."

"We all just need to commit to promoting these items, by using them more often," Energia replied diligently and pleadingly.

"I will be mindful, and I promise to spread the good news around," Yema said with a gracious nod.

Another guest, Mr. Dudu, Oxwe's friend and groomsman, would confess to the bridegroom and the bride gratefully, "The meal was both tasty and healthy, I have eaten to satiety."

The newlyweds were glad to hear and know their friends had enjoyed the food. They would publicly express their gratitude and appreciation to Mrs. Zan and her team through a big round of applause.

After cutting the wedding cake, the two guests of honor would go to the podium for some dance together.

While climbing onto the podium alongside Oxwe, with their arms intertwined, Energia whispered into her husband's ears, "Honey, I do not think I can compete with you on this stage."

"Darling, you certainly can do it, I have seen you in action," he replied, while giggling.

At the beat of the music, the newlyweds hit the floor with amazing dance steps, with a standing ovation from the audience. Many friends would join them on the podium to dance happily in support of the new spouses. It all happened in a lively, relaxed, and romantic ambiance.

Following the wedding ceremony and reception, the couple quietly withdrew to their new home in Djehon on a horse-drawn coach.

The newly married couple had bought a house in Djehon to live together and raise a family. The materials used in building their newly purchased house met the standards and requirements of renewable energy. The house ran entirely on a combination of solar panels and wind energy. The backyard was full of beautiful trees, coming in all shapes and sizes. Lana, a neighbor once suggested that the backyard resembled a dense forest; it featured an amalgam of trees reflecting some lovely foliage. Energia would encourage her new neighbors not to cut down trees in the neighborhood.

A neighbor named Osab was once cutting down a big and shady tree in front of his house, while Energia and Oxwe were walking by for a routine exercise on a Saturday morning. She reached out to the neighbor and asked him politely, "Excuse me, sir! Have you planted another tree before cutting down this one?"

"No," he replied sharply, "these trees can be cumbersome sometimes."

"Trees are never cumbrous, we need them for the health of the earth and for our health," she replied gently.

"In the future, please remember to never cut down a tree without first planting a new one to replace the old one," she added, pleading the case for trees.

"Understood, madam, and thank you!" he exclaimed.

"By the way, my name is Osab," he went on kindly.

"Nice to meet you! My name is Energia, and this is my husband Oxwe".

"We are new in the neighborhood," Oxwe added humbly.

"Wow, it is great to meet you. I heard great things about you, madam, all your great achievements for clean energy and healthy environment," Osab said with excitement.

"Welcome to the neighborhood," he continued, "it is a quiet and friendly neighborhood, and your addition will make it better and healthier. Happy to have you in our neighborhood!"

"Thank you!" Energia replied before bidding goodbye to Osab.

That encounter and conversation occurred on a morning in April; it was a friendly interaction.

Three months later, on a hot summer day, Energia and Oxwe were walking by again, while Osab was planting young trees in the front yard of his house.

As soon as he saw the couple, Osab dropped everything and reached out to greet them.

"Good morning, Oxwe and Energia!" he said candidly.

"Good morning, Osab! It is nice to see you again!" they replied promptly.

And they stopped to chat for a while.

"Energia was right, I feel more heat by my front yard this year, more so than before, when my old tree was here," Osab complained profoundly. "I now know that cutting down the shady tree was not a good idea."

"I had anticipated this problem," Energia replied softly.

"Plus, my birds are all gone since I cut down that tree," he added remorsefully. "I no longer see any bird around my house. I love birds, and I enjoy watching them. They used to spend time around, on the tree and under its shade, they would build their nests on its branches to rest, to lay eggs and shelter their young. I miss them very much!"

"The human species certainly needs the inspiring presence, the fascinating movements, and the beautiful sounds of birds around us," Energia said patiently. "I hope you have learned your lesson."

"It is a good sign you are planting new trees!" Oxwe exclaimed optimistically.

"Yes, that is encouraging!" Energia added plainly.

"I really appreciate your kind advice, it is motivating, and I am very grateful! Thank you," Osab said before heading back to planting his young trees, while Energia and Oxwe continued their walk in the neighborhood.

In a different situation, when another neighbor named Konu challenged Energia and Oxwe to cut down some trees to clear some space in their backyard, Oxwe responded didactically, "Why should I cut down any of these magnificent and beneficent trees, when I know they help me cool off and feel better?"

"That is probably correct," Konu replied, "it is a fact that anytime I stop by your backyard, it feels cooler than my own backyard."

"I have only a few trees in my backyard, and it feels hot. I may need to reconsider and plant more trees," he went on curiously.

"That is right," Energia interrupted with a smile, "there is a secret in planting more trees; the more trees we grow, the better our bodies feel."

A year later, Energia gave birth to their beautiful daughter Ifae. Three years later, their handsome son Olo was born. The children would grow up physically and mentally in a happy and healthy environment of clean energy; they would mature spiritually and emotionally under the watch of responsible parents. While raising their family, the couple in their lifestyle was mindful of preserving a green and healthy earth for their children's generation and for all future generations. Energia gave up her cars and opted for a horse as her main mode of transport. She was happier riding a horse to go to work. Oxwe also adopted a horse and a bicycle as his new means of transportation. He would alternate between riding a bicycle and horseback riding to travel back and forth to his workplace.

Energia would seize the occasion of Ifae's seventh birthday bash to say to all the children gathered for the event: "The most helpful and meaningful legacy our generation could leave to future generations would be a green earth with clean air; that is the safest legacy."

The children did not understand fully what she meant, but they all gracefully gave her a standing ovation.

She would also use the opportunity of the birthday party to coach them with some guidelines she thought of as golden rules for the youth in that context.

"Remember," she said to them, "remember to always turn off the light when there is nobody in the room; do not use or play with plastic bags; do not use a straw to sip your beverage; do not litter, for littering is an insult to the earth. If you make a mess, clean it patiently and gently."

"Every clean initiative or act helps and reflects our good will to save our planet," she added to conclude her series of lessons to the children.

"Thank you, Mommy, for your kind advice to me and my friends!" Ifae exclaimed shortly afterward.

Ten years after their marriage, Oxwe abandoned his lucrative profession of a chief information officer, and he got involved in politics. He ran a tremendous campaign on renewable energy for all and won a seat in the powerful parliament of the kingdom of Energium to promote legislations of clean energy. Alongside his wife's initiatives and efforts, as a member of the parliament, he dynamically introduced and helped pass several bills on renewable energy. Under his leadership, as the head of the national assembly, the parliament adopted a series of significant legislations for the promotion and sustainability of wind and solar energy in Energium and beyond the kingdom.

Energia was very pleased with her husband's achievements. He was equally very satisfied with his wife's accomplishments. While the couple celebrated their successes with mutual gratitude, they were also mindful to support each other in times of failures and contradictions. They would collaborate tirelessly on several related fronts to help mitigate global warming and climate change, by working to reduce the greenhouse gas emissions to redeem our planet, for the sake of humankind.

To commemorate their fifteenth anniversary, the couple would use the opportunity of a summer vacation for a week-long spiritual retreat. They withdrew from their activities and from the city to the remote and quiet location of a monastery for self-examination, to evaluate their progress and their shortcomings in the daily life and activities.

After spending their first day of retreat in a contemplative meditation on the beauty and greatness of the universe, Oxwe and Energia reflected on their contemplation around the dining table.

Oxwe said meditatively: "When I contemplate the beautiful vegetation around me, with these majestic green trees dancing to the rhythm of the breeze, and the great variety of animals wandering enthusiastically in the forests, when I consider the splendor of the gorgeous waterfalls around here, when I watch the agility of the lovely birds flying happily in the sky, and the movements of the fish playing in the river running by, when I look at the crabs walking cleverly on the beach nearby, when I think of the amazing succession of the seasons and the mystery and beauty of the human body, it all reminds me we are the guardians of the treasure the earth represents, and I feel humble, as I measure the magnitude and value of that responsibility."

"Yes," Energia said spontaneously, "the human species could be more mindful we are the caretakers of this pearl called earth. It is our primordial and primo responsibility to protect and preserve our precious planet by all means; we need not to waste or destroy the earth with immoderate ambitions."

As they thought deeply about their life together and their activities, Energia acknowledged that the road ahead remained long. She would confide to Oxwe carefully, "We still have a long way to go in our journey to curb the greenhouse gas emissions and to mitigate global warming and climate change."

The husband would creatively find a realistic way to empower his wife meaningfully.

"Be mindful that every positive action or initiative represents a significant step toward achieving the green goal," Oxwe replied confidently, before adding, "There is no doubt it is a long journey! A senseless addiction to the fossil fuels has driven the earth into a very dark tunnel. Our stubbornness, or our slowness in taking decisive reversible actions to counter the trending behaviors in the mainstream, only maintains the earth in the tunnel, far away from its end. But our willingness to meet and talk over a possible course of constructive actions portrays a glimmer of hope on the horizon."

"Yes, there certainly is hope, we are on the right track!" Energia exclaimed agreeably. "Our small initiatives give us good reasons to believe there is a light at the end of the tunnel."

INDEX

Q

qualitative design ix
qualitative research ix, 22, 44
qualitative research methods ix
quality of sleep 7
quantitative procedures ix
quantitative research ix, x, 22, 107
quantitative research methods ix
quarantine 5, 7
questionnaire 64–65, 67–69

R

radioactive materials 74
random assignment 58–60
random sample 50, 74
random selection 59–60
ranking 25, 89–90
raw data 99
reciprocity 23–24, 66, 69
refereed journals 16
reforestation 111, 113, 116
regression analysis ix, 80, 88, 90–93,
    96–99
relationship v, 8, 60, 71, 88–91, 94–
    95, 116, 118
reliability x, 39, 65, 68, 106–107, 113
religion 25
Remo platform 6
renewable energies ix, x, 11–14, 18–21,
    37, 78–79, 106, 110
research advisor 13, 19, 40
research consultant 13
research cultures ix
researchers 24, 26–27, 54–55, 106
research experts 16
research methodologies ix, x,
research methods ix, x, 20, 107, 137
research process ix, 14, 17, 22–24, 27,
    40, 44, 52, 106
research project 20, 26
research proposal 20–21, 25

research question 14–15, 19, 60
research strategist 57
residents 7, 31, 33–34, 37–38, 58, 67,
    69, 72, 113
respect 6, 23–24, 39, 88, 108
respiratory diseases 4, 116
respondents 22–23, 52, 66, 69–70,
    74, 81
results 15–17, 22, 46, 50, 52, 62–64,
    66, 68–69, 72, 74, 79, 82,
    84–87, 94–97, 99, 101–103,
    105–107, 110, 112, 114–116
river 10, 42, 51, 54, 57, 67, 125
rivers 10, 50, 64
rural areas 7
rural communities 4

S

sample size 15, 17–18, 107, 113
sampling technique 15, 18
sampling techniques 17
scapegoating 12
scholarly articles 16, 19
scholarly evidence 21
schools 5–6, 36, 39, 44
scientific advancements 11
scientific discoveries x, 106
scientific investigations x, 106
scope x, 68, 107
seawaters 51
self-evaluation 1
self-examination ix, 1, 3, 7, 9, 13–14,
    124, 137
self-reflection 8
semi-structured interviews 51
significance x, 21, 94, 101, 113
Simple Scatter 94
Simple Scatterplot 94
single group experiment 60
Skype 6
Slack 6

ABOUT THE AUTHOR

Dr. Jacques L. Koko is an associate professor of conflict analysis and dispute resolution and graduate program director at Salisbury University in Maryland. His focus includes organizational conflict management and leadership development, cross-cultural conflict resolution, religion for conflict transformation, conflicts relating to global warming and climate change, conflict coaching, effective communication in the workplace, group facilitation, family therapy, peacemaking (meditation, self-examination, negotiation and mediation), peacekeeping, peacebuilding, and research methods in conflict transformation.

Lightning Source UK Ltd.
Milton Keynes UK
UKHW042105031122
411597UK00001B/206

9 798765 227794